NCERT PRACTICE

Work BOOK

Science

Class 7

Hundreds of Practice Questions; MCQs, Fill in the Blanks, True-False, Matching, VSA, SA, LA, etc.

arihant
Arihant Prakashan (School Division Series)

arihant
Arihant Prakashan (School Division Series)

Administrative & Production Offices

Regd. Office
'Ramchhaya' 4577/15, Agarwal Road, Darya Ganj, New Delhi -110002
Tele: 011- 47630600, 43518550

Head Office
Kalindi, TP Nagar, Meerut (UP) - 250002
Tel: 0121-7156203, 7156204

Sales & Support Offices
Agra, Ahmedabad, Bengaluru, Bareilly, Chennai, Delhi, Guwahati, Hyderabad, Jaipur, Jhansi, Kolkata, Lucknow, Nagpur & Pune.

PRICE ₹ 125.00

PO No : TXT-XX-XXXXXXX-X-XX

Published by Arihant Publications (India) Ltd.

For further information about the books published by Arihant, log on to www.arihantbooks.com or e-mail at info@arihantbooks.com

Follow us on

9789327196955

PRODUCTION TEAM

Publishing Managers
Mahendra Singh Rawat
Keshav Mohan

Project Coordinator
Akansha Tomar

Project Editor
Satyam Kumar

Cover Designer
Bilal Hashmi

Inner Designer
Ankit Saini

Proof Readers
Sarthak Sharma

Workbook, Why?

"Knowledge will not be with you for Long Unless You Practice "

This quotation answer the above question 'Workbook,Why ?' perfectly,the explanation is given in the text given below.

NCERT textbooks are the only textbooks, which have been prepared according to National Curriculum Framework, which discourages the idea of rote learning and recommends that students' life at school must be linked to their life outside the school. NCERT textbooks don't emphasize on remembering concepts rather they focus on understanding and try to make the students able to identify the way of problem solving.

ONLY WORKBOOK BASED ON NCERT

Keeping the importance of NCERT textbooks in mind we have prepared this Workbook, strictly based on NCERT content, this Workbook will complement NCERT by providing practice to help reinforce the material given in each chapter of NCERT textbook.

WORKBOOK– PURPOSE, USE & FEATURES

This Workbook, through its numerous exercises having different variety of questions covering each and every fact of NCERT, will prove to be equally useful for both, Classroom and at Home. One more purpose of this Workbook is to provide the students a systematic practice of the content taught in the class and what they study in the textbooks.

Some special features of this workbook are

- Topical division of each chapter for complete practice.
- Different variety of questions; Fill in the Blanks, True-False, Matching, Multiple Choice Questions, Differentiate between, Define the following, One word for, Odd One Out, Very Short Answer, Short Answer, Long Answer Type, etc.
- Alongwith Topical Worksheets, complete worksheet for the chapter as whole, at the end of the chapter.

WORKBOOK– DESIGNED TO IMPROVE SUBJECT ABILITIES

All the material given in this workbook is tailored to suit subject content with equal support on learning, which will surely help students to boost their abilities and confidence in the subject.

We look forward for the feedback from students,teachers and parents for the further improvement of the contents of this book. We will try to update the contents according to your feedback in further editions of this Workbook.

The Publisher

Contents

[Chapter 1]

Nutrition in Plants

Worksheet 1 Autotrophic Nutrition in Plants

Multiple Choice Questions (MCQs)

1 The process of taking in food by an organism and its utilisation by the body is called

(a) eating (b) respiration (c) nutrition (d) digestion

2 Plants can be categorised as

(a) heterotrophs (b) autotrophs

(c) saprotrophs (d) parasite

3 When we observe the lower surface of a leaf through a magnifying lens we see numerous small openings. Which of the following is the term given to such openings?

(a) Stomata (b) Lamina (c) Midrib (d) Veins

4 Which of the following is absorbed from the air by plants through stomata?

I. Water II. Nitrogen

III. Carbohydrates IV. Carbon dioxide

Choose the correct option:

(a) Both I and II (b) Both II and III

(c) Both III and IV (d) Only IV

5 In the absence of which of the following photosynthesis will not occur in leaves?

(a) Oxygen (b) Chlorophyll

(c) Vacuole (d) Space between cell

6 In a cactus plant, food is made by

I. branches II. roots

III. leaves IV. stem

Choose the correct option:

(a) Both I and II (b) Both II and III

(c) Both III and IV (d) Only IV

Fill in the Blanks

1 Fill in the blanks by using the suitable word given in the bracket:

(a) All animals are categorised as __________. (autotrophs/heterotrophs)

(b) The food making process in plants is called __________. (transpiration/photosynthesis)

(c) __________ (Chlorophyll / Stomata) is the site of reception of light energy in leaves.

(d) The nucleus is surrounded by a jelly-like substance called __________. (cytoplasm/protein)

(e) __________ (Fats / Carbohydrates) are made up of carbon, hydrogen and oxygen.

(f) Plants cannot absorb __________. (carbon dioxide/nitrogen)

True/False

1 Write 'T' for True or 'F' for False for the following statements:

(a) Carbohydrates and proteins can be called as nutrients.

(b) The synthesis of food in plants occurs in roots.

(c) Cells have a centrally located spherical structure called nucleus.

(d) Pores on the leaves are surrounded by cell membrane.

(e) During photosynthesis, oxygen is absorbed.

(f) Desert plants have spines to reduce photosynthesis.

(g) Plants can also synthesise proteins and fats.

Matching Type

1 Match the following raw materials of photosynthesis in column I with the place where they are available in column II:

Column I (*Raw material of photosynthesis*)	**Column II** (*Place*)
(a) Sunlight	(i) Available in the air
(b) Chlorophyll	(ii) Available in the plant
(c) Carbon dioxide	(iii) Available in the soil
(d) Water	(iv) Available during the day
(e) Minerals	

Define the following terms:

1 Autotrophic nutrition

____

2 Cell

____

3 Cell membrane

4 Chlorophyll

5 Starch

6 Photosynthesis

Differentiate between the following:

1 Stomata and Guard cells

2 Plants and Lichens

Very Short Answer Type Questions

1 Name the type of energy captured by the leaves to form food.

2 Label the parts *A*, *B* and *C* in the figure:

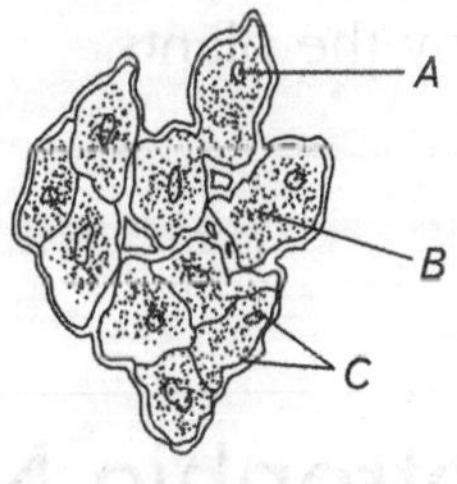

Cell

3 Correct the incorrectly labelled parts in the figure of section of a leaf below:

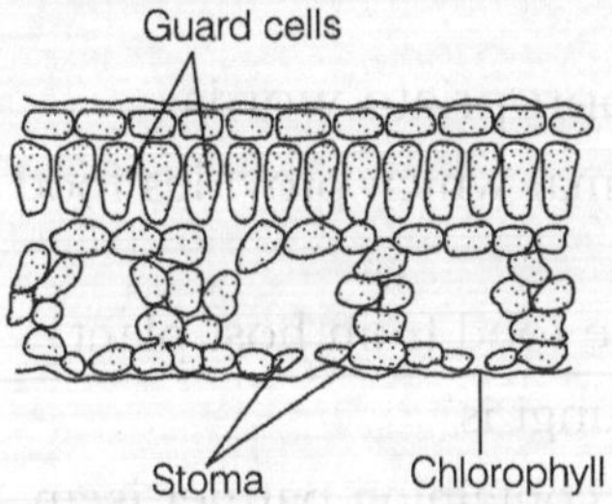

A section of a leaf

Short Answer Type Questions

1 How are water and minerals transported to the leaves?

2 A person observes some plants having deep red, violet and brown coloured leaves. Can these leaves carry out photosynthesis? Give reason for your answer.

Long Answer Type Questions

1 (a) Why cannot our body make food from CO_2, H_2O and minerals like plants?

(b) How do plants obtain the raw materials necessary for photosynthesis from the surroundings?

2 State the importance of photosynthesis and write the overall chemical equation for the process.

3 Explain the uptake of nitrogen by the plants.

Worksheet 2 Heterotrophic Nutrition and Nutrient Replenishment in Soil

Fill in the Blanks

1 Fill in the blanks with the appropriate words:

(a) The green plant or the animal which provides food in a relationship is called the ________.

(b) Plants like ________ take food from host plant.

(c) The mode of nutrition in fungi is ________.

(d) In lichens, the chlorophyll containing partner is an ________.

(e) ________ contain plant nutrients like nitrogen, potassium, etc.

(f) ________ converts atmospheric nitrogen into a soluble form.

True/False

1 Write 'T' for True or 'F' for False for the following statements:

(a) Only animals can be called as parasites. ☐

(b) Non-green plants perform heterotrophic mode of nutrition. ☐

(c) *Cuscuta* takes readymade food from the plant on which it is climbing. ☐

(d) *Rhizobium* is a fungus which absorbs nitrogen from the air. ☐

(e) Leguminous plants do not need nitrogenous fertilisers. ☐

Multiple Choice Questions (MCQs)

1 Pitcher plant traps insects because it

(a) is a heterotroph

(b) has to fulfil its nutrition requirements

(c) does not have chlorophyll

(d) has a digestive system like human beings

2 Refer to the given figure. It illustrates

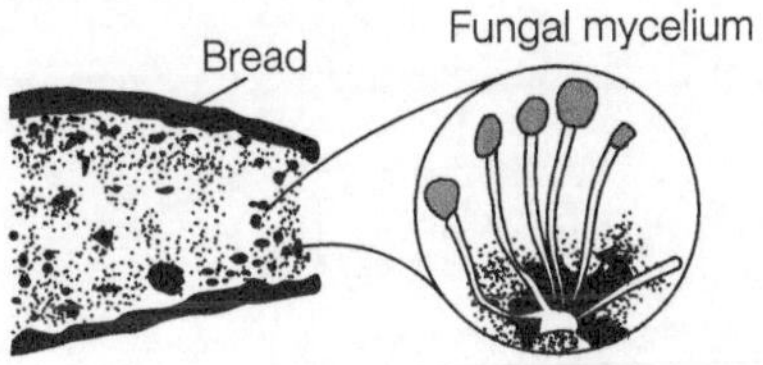

(a) Autotrophic nutrition
(b) Saprotrophic nutrition
(c) Parasitic nutrition
(d) Symbiotic nutrition

3 With which of thc following, *Rhizobium* can form a symbiotic association?

I. Gram II. Beans III. Mango IV. Mustard

Choose the correct option:

(a) Both I and II
(b) Both II and III
(c) Both III and IV
(d) Both I and IV

Define the following terms:

1 Heterotrophic nutrition

2 Insectivorous plants

3 Saprotrophs

4 Symbiotic relationship

Very Short Answer Type Questions

1 Give two examples of each:

(a) Useful fungi

(b) Leguminous plants

2 *Cuscuta* takes readymade food from the plant on which it is climbing. What general name is given to such plants? Name the plant from which it gets nutrition.

Short Answer Type Questions

1 (a) Draw a diagram of a pitcher plant showing lid and pitcher.

(b) Is it an autotroph or partial heterotroph?

2 What are the characteristic of fungi? Also, write about their mode of nutrition.

Long Answer Type Questions

1 Describe the mechanism by which a pitcher plant derives its nourishment.

2 What is a lichen? How does it survive?

3 Explain the symbiotic association of *Rhizobium* and pea plant. Also, state its importance for the farmers.

SUMMATIVE ASSESSMENT

BASED ON COMPLETE CHAPTER .....

Multiple Choice Questions (MCQs) (1 mark each)

1 Which of the following statements is/are correct?

I. All green plants can prepare their own food.

II. Most animals are autotrophs.

III. Carbon dioxide is not required for photosynthesis.

IV. Oxygen is liberated during photosynthesis.

Choose the correct option:

(a) Both I and IV (b) Only II

(c) Both II and III (d) Both I and II

2 Which of the following can grow on leather, clothes, etc. that are left in hot and humid weather for a long time?

(a) Algae (b) Fungi (c) Mushrooms (d) *Cuscuta*

3 The bacterium *Rhizobium* helps some of the crops to get nitrogen. Which of the following statement is incorrect for *Rhizobium*?

(a) It converts atmospheric nitrogen into a soluble form that the plants can absorb.

(b) It can make its own food.

(c) It lives in the roots of leguminous plants like grams, peas, *moong*, etc.

(d) Leguminous plants provide food and shelter to *Rhizobium*.

4 During photosynthesis

(a) solar energy is converted into chemical energy

(b) solar energy is converted into mechanical energy

(c) chemical energy is converted into mechanical energy

(d) bioenergy is converted into chemical energy

5 Insectivorous plants eat insects to fulfil their needs of

(a) energy (b) nitrogen (c) phosphorus (d) potassium

Very Short Answer Type Questions (1 mark each)

1 Which mineral is needed by plants to make protein?

2 Name a plant in which photosynthesis occurs in plant part other than leaves.

3 Name the form in which the food synthesised by plants is stored.

4 Name the parasite plant with a yellow, slender and tubular stem.

5 What is the relationship between an alga and a fungus in lichens called?

Short Answer Type I Questions (2 marks each)

1 Organisms like mosquitoes, bed bugs, lice and leeches suck our blood. Are they also considered parasites?

2 What is so special about leaves that they can synthesise food?

Short Answer Type II Questions (3 marks each)

1 Explain the structure of a cell as seen under the microscope.

2 Give reasons to support the statement: In the absence of photosynthesis, life would be impossible on Earth.

Long Answer Type Questions (5 marks each)

1 The figure given below shows an experimental set up:

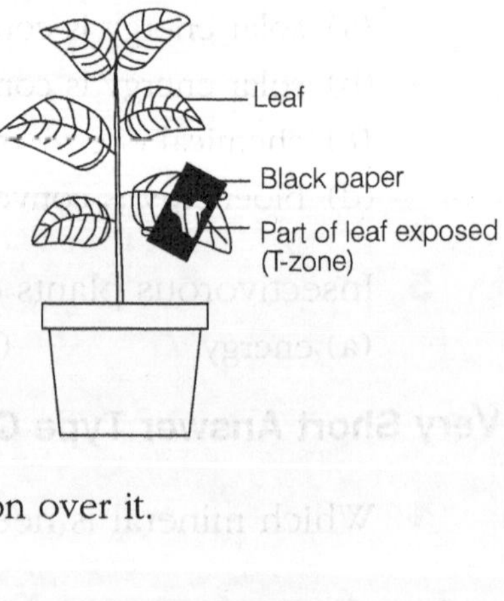

(a) Following are the steps needed to do a starch test but in random order:

(i) Pluck a leaf from the plant.

(ii) Leave the potted plant out in the sun for a few hour.

(iii) Boil the leaf in alcohol.

(iv) Boil the leaf in water.

(v) Wash the leaf and then add a few drops of iodine solution over it.

Arrange these steps in correct order:

(b) After adding iodine colour change in parts *A*, *B* and *C* of the leaf is seen. Give reason for the observation.

(i) Part *A* ____________________

(ii) Part *B* ____________________

(iii) Part *C* ____________________

2 How are nutrients replenished in the soil?

____

____

ACTIVITY (Word Search)

Spot as many organisms as possible in the puzzle given in figure by encircling them as shown. Write the names on a sheet of paper and categorise them into autotrophs and heterotrophs. Classify the heterotrophs into herbivores, carnivores, omnivores and saprophytes.

B	R	O	S	E	A	T	C	R	O	W
A	A	G	N	B	H	I	N	D	I	B
N	B	N	G	I	N	G	E	R	C	L
Y	B	A	N	H	B	E	C	O	W	F
A	I	M	U	S	H	R	O	O	M	F
N	T	G	B	E	R	M	W	F	I	O
E	L	E	P	H	A	N	T	S	C	X
T	S	A	E	Y	N	P	H	B	E	E
C	A	R	R	O	T	U	L	S	I	X

Chapter 2

Nutrition in Animals

Worksheet 1 Digestion in Humans

Matching Type

1 Match the animals in column I with their mode of feeding listed in column II:

Column I (*Animals*)	**Column II** (*Mode of feeding*)
(a) Eagle	(i) Swallowing
(b) Snake	(ii) Sucking
(c) Snail	(iii) Tearing
(d) Infants	(iv) Scraping

Multiple Choice Questions (MCQs)

1 In grinding, food is acted upon by

(a) teeth and saliva (b) jaws and tongue (c) lips and saliva (d) lips and tongue

2 The upper jaw of the human adult contains

(a) 4 incisors, 2 canines, 4 premolars and 6 molars

(b) 4 incisors, 4 canines, 4 premolars and 4 molars

(c) 8 incisors, 2 canines, 2 premolars and 4 molars

(d) 4 incisors, 4 canines, 2 premolars and 6 molars

3 Digestive juices are secreted by

I. liver II. pancreas III. salivary glands

IV. stomach V. intestine

Choose the correct option:

(a) Both I and II (b) Both III and IV (c) Both II and V (d) All of these

4 The digestion of a particular food in the small intestine produces amino acids. This food must be containing mainly

(a) carbohydrates (b) fats (c) vitamins (d) proteins

5 Proper care of the teeth helps to

(a) prevent tooth decay
(b) prevent dental plaque
(c) prevent tooth loss
(d) All of these

6 The digestion of groundnut oil, present in food produces

I. amino acid
II. glycerol
III. alcohol
IV. fatty acid

Choose the correct option:

(a) Both I and II
(b) Both II and III
(c) Both III and IV
(d) Both II and IV

Fill in the Blanks

1 Fill in the blanks with the appropriate words:

(a) The alimentary canal stretches from ________ to ________.
(b) Digestion of food starts in ________ and gets completed in ________.
(c) Teeth are rooted in separate ________ in between the ________.
(d) Tongue is attached at the ________ to the floor of mouth cavity and is free at the ________.
(e) Large intestine absorbs ________ and some ________ from the undigested food.

2 Read the given paragraph carefully and fill in the blanks from the words given in the box:

liver	*gall bladder*	*glycerol*	*fatty acids*	*fats*

The ______(a)______ secretes the bile juice which is stored in the ______(b)______. The bile breaks up ______(c)______ into tiny droplets that can be digested and absorbed more easily. The digestive juices then act on these tiny droplets to form simpler compounds known as ______(d)______ and ______(e)______.

True/False

1 Write 'T' for True or 'F' for False for the following statements:

(a) The mode of feeding of eagle is capturing and swallowing. ☐
(b) All heterotrophs have a similar basic process of nutrition. ☐
(c) The food is grinded by the contraction and expansion of villi. ☐
(d) Salivary glands release hydrochloric acid. ☐
(e) Iodine can turn starch solution red. ☐
(f) Glycerol is one of the digested product of fats. ☐
(g) The large intestine is longer and wider than the small intestine of the human alimentary canal. ☐
(h) Complete digestion of fats takes place in large intestine. ☐

Answer the following statements in one word:

1 Another name for food pipe.

2 Teeth present in infants.

3 An instant source of energy.

Differentiate between the following:

1 Liver and Pancreas

2 Small intestine and Large intestine

3 Milk teeth and Permanent teeth

4 Digestion and Absorption

Define the following terms:

1 Buccal cavity

2 Nutrition in animals

3 Digestive tract

4 Egestion

5 Assimilation

6 Ingestion

Give reasons for the following:

1 The swallowed food moves downward in the alimentary canal.

2 Hydrochloric acid in the stomach does not digest its own inner lining.

3 Eating lots of chocolates and sweets causes tooth decay.

Very Short Answer Type Questions

1 Choose odd one out and justify the correct choice:

(a) Oesophagus, large intestine, small intestine, rectum

(b) Gastric juice, pancreatic juice, hydrochloric acid, glycerol

2 Name the condition in which a person passes out frequent watery stools.

Short Answer Type Questions

1 What is the action of saliva on our food?

2 State the various functions of the tongue. Name four different tastes which can be detected by our tongue.

3 What is tooth decay? How can you prevent it?

4 Given below is a diagram showing the human digestive system. Correctly label its incorrectly labelled parts and other missing parts.

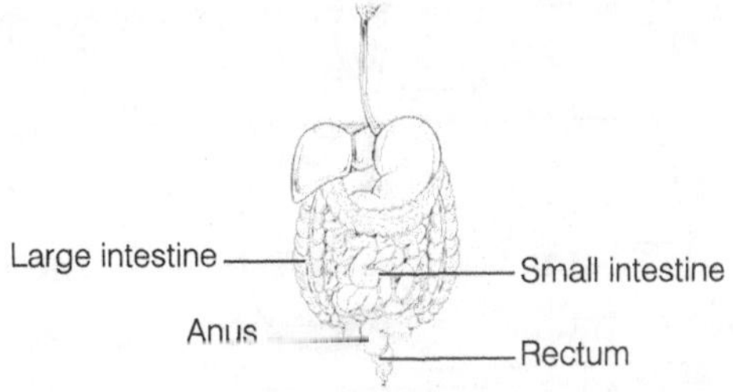

Long Answer Type Questions

1 Describe absorption in the small intestine with reference to the working of villi.

2 What is meant by digestion? Name the various organs of the human digestive system and their respective functions.

3 Observe the figure given below of the four different types of teeth in human. Name them and also write their function.

Teeth	Name	Function

4 What is diarrhoea and how it is caused? What is the first step of treatment of diarrhoea at home?

5 Look at the figure below and write about the processes taking place during passage of food in various parts. Also label the parts *A*, *B* and *C*.

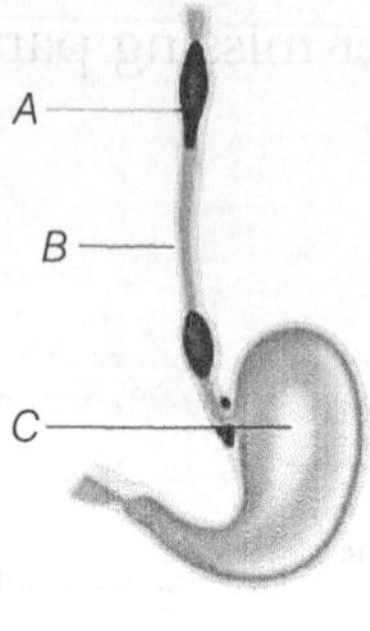

Worksheet 2 Digestion in Animals

Multiple Choice Questions (MCQs)

1 A part of stomach where food is stored in a cattle is

(a) oesophagus (b) caecum

(c) rumen (d) intestine

2 Cud is the name given to the food of ruminants which is

(a) swallowed and undigested

(b) swallowed and partially digested

(c) properly chewed and partially digested

(d) properly chewed and completely digested

3 Which of the following can digest cellulose, a type of carbohydrate present in its food?

(a) Cow (b) Lion (c) Cat (d) Man

True/False

1 Following are the statements related to *Amoeba*. State True (T) or False (F) against each statement:

(a) *Amoeba* is a microscopic, multicellular organism. ☐

(b) The most important feature of *Amoeba* is that it has no fixed shape. ☐

(c) Food vacuole in *Amoeba* is used for both digestion and egestion. ☐

(d) *Amoeba* engulfs its food through its nucleus. ☐

Fill in the Blanks

1 Given below is a paragraph related to digestive system of a cow. Fill in the blanks by using the suitable words from the box:

bacteria	*ruminant*	*caecum*
large intestine	*humans*	*cellulose*

Cow is a ______(a)______ which has a large sac-like structure called ______(b)______ between small intestine and ______(c)______. The ______(d)______ of the food is digested here by the action of certain ______(e)______ which are not present in other animals like ______(f)______.

Matching Type

1 Match the organs in column I with the words listed in column II:

Column I (*Organ*)	Column II (*Word*)
(a) Rectum	(i) Mucous
(b) Gall bladder	(ii) Villi
(c) Stomach	(iii) Taste buds
(d) Tongue	(iv) Faeces
(e) Small intestine	(v) Bile juice

Define the following terms:

1 Cud

2 Ruminants

3 Rumination

Very Short Answer Type Questions

1 What is the importance of rumen?

2 What are the false feet of *Amoeba* known as?

3 Name the site of secretion of digestive juices in the body of *Amoeba*.

Short Answer Type Questions

1 Animals such as cows can digest grass but humans cannot. Do you agree? Give reasons.

2 Given below is the diagram of a cow. Draw its digestive system and label its parts:

Long Answer Type Questions

1 Describe the process of nutrition in ruminants.

2 Explain the process of digestion and absorption in *Amoeba* with diagram.

SUMMATIVE ASSESSMENT

BASED ON COMPLETE CHAPTER .....

Multiple Choice Questions (MCQs) (1 mark each)

1 The five steps of nutrition are given below. Put them in correct order.

I. Assimilation II. Ingestion III. Egestion

IV. Digestion V. Absorption

Choose the correct option:

(a) I, IV, III, V and II (b) II, V, III, I and III

(c) II, IV, V, I and III (d) IV, I, V, II and III

2 Read the following statements with reference to the villi of small intestine.

I. They have very thin walls.

II. They have a network of thin and small blood vessels close to the surface.

III. They have small pores through which food can easily pass.

IV. They are finger-like projections.

Identify those statements which enable the villi to absorb digested food.

(a) I, II and IV (b) II, III and IV (c) III and IV (d) I and IV

3 The given figure shows a *Amoeba* with its various parts. Identify the incorrectly labelled part.

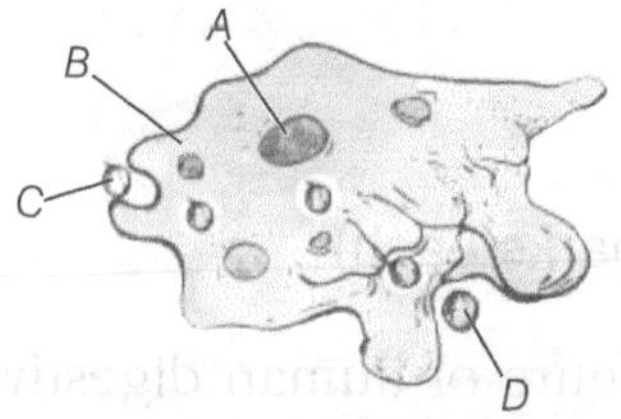

(a) *A*-Food vacuole (b) *B*-Pseudopodium

(c) *C*-Food particle (d) *D*-Egested waste

4 A proboscis is present in

(a) housefly (b) cockroach (c) butterfly (d) lizard

5 Which of the following are called the tearing teeth?

(a) Incisors (b) Canines (c) Molars (d) Premolars

Very Short Answer Type Questions (1 mark each)

1 Why does bread taste sweet on mastication?

2 What carries food to stomach from mouth?

3 What are permanent teeth?

4 What happens when glucose is broken down in body cells of animals with the help of oxygen?

5 Name the food items that are a cause of tooth decay.

Short Answer Type I Questions (2 marks each)

1 What is the role of villi in the small intestine?

2 Why have the ruminants developed the habit of 'chewing cud'?

Short Answer Type II Questions (3 marks each)

1 Write a note on the discovery of working of stomach.

2 Sometimes when we are having a meal, we feel choked, get hiccups or start coughing. Why?

Long Answer Type Questions (5 marks each)

1 Label the parts in the given figure of human digestive system and write the characteristic feature of each of them.

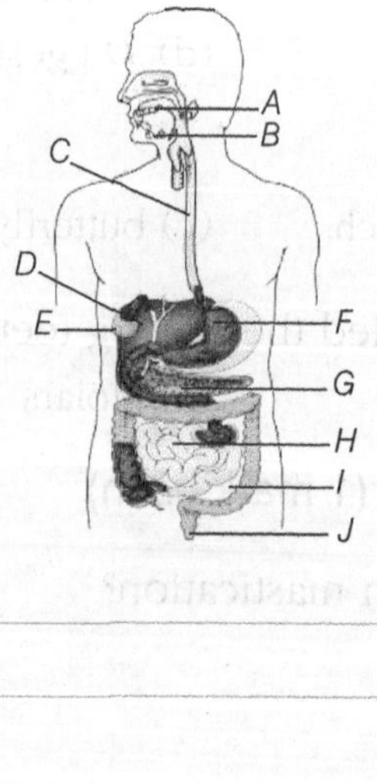

2 Read the following passage carefully and answer the questions that follow it.

Bile juice is stored in a sac called, gall bladder, located near its organ of secretion, liver . The gall bladder releases the bile juice into the small intestine whenever food reaches there. Though bile juice is devoid of any digestive enzymes, it is required for the digestion of fats.

The fats cannot be digested easily because they are insoluble in water and are present as large globules. Bile juice breaks down the big fat droplets into smaller droplets. These are then easily digested by the enzymes released from the pancreas.

(a) Which organ secretes the bile juice?

____

____

(b) Why is digestion of fats difficult as compared to that of other nutrients?

____

____

(c) How does bile juice help in digestion of fat?

____

____

(d) Where is the digestion of fat completed?

____

____

(e) Does bile juice digest fat completely?

____

____

ACTIVITY (Crossword)

Complete the crossword with the help of clues given below:

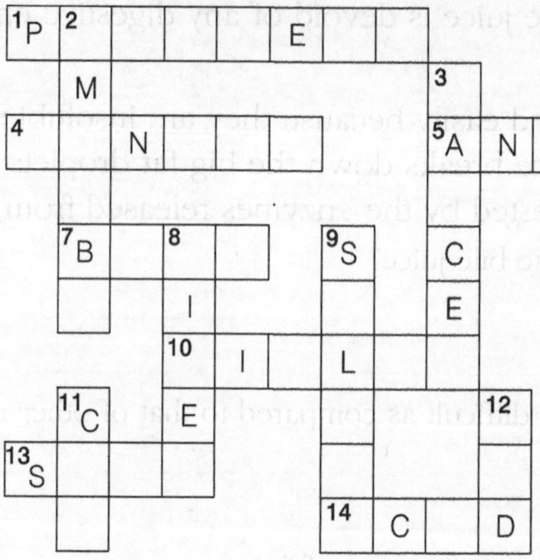

Across

1. Cream-coloured digestive gland
4. Organ that mixes saliva with the food
5. Point of defecation
7. Stored in gall bladder
10. Finger-like outgrowth in the small intestine
13. A kind of taste bud
14. Kills bacteria in the stomach

Down

2. Feeds with the help of pseudopodia
3. Undigested excretory solid residues
6. Total number of molars in one jaw of an adult
8. The largest gland
9. Watery secretion in the mouth
11. A ruminant
12. Form of food chewed by ruminants

Chapter 3

Fibre to Fabric

Worksheet 1 Animal Fibre-Wool

Multiple Choice Questions (MCQs)

1 Which part of the sheep's fleece is used for making wool?
(a) Coarse beard hair (b) Soft under hair close to skin
(c) Both (a) and (b) (d) None of these

2 Which one of the following is not a breed of sheep?
(a) Murrah (b) Marwari (c) Nali (d) Lohi

3 The hair of sheep is removed only once a year before the beginning of
(a) spring season (b) summer season
(c) rainy season (d) winter season

True/False

1 Write 'T' for True or 'F' for False for the following statements:
(a) Shearing does not cause any pain to the sheep. ☐
(b) Nali breed of sheep is found in the state of Jammu and Kashmir. ☐
(c) Yak hair are not used to make woollen fabric. ☐
(d) Pashmina shawl woven from the wool are obtained from the under fur of Kashmiri goats. ☐
(e) The process of selecting parents for obtaining special characters in their offspring is called selective breeding. ☐

Fill in the Blanks

1 Complete the following table with the help of words given in the two categories:

Name of breed	Quality of wool
A. Bakharwal	I. Coarse wool
B. Rampur bushair	II. Carpet wool
C. Lohi	III. Good quality wool
D. Patanwadi	IV. For Pashmina shawls

Name of breed	Quality of wool	State where found
Lohi	(a)__________	Rajasthan, Punjab
(b)__________	Brown fleece	Uttar Pradesh
Nali	(c)__________	Haryana, Punjab
(d)__________	For woollen shawls	Jammu and Kashmir
Marwari	(e)__________	Gujarat
(f)__________	Hosiery	Gujarat

2 Fill in the blanks with the help of words given in the box:

hazards	*virus*	*bacterium*	*respiratory disease*	*sorter's disease*
anthrax	*scabies*	*occupational*	*traditional*	

Wool industry is an important means of livelihood for many people in our country. But sorter's job is risky as sometimes they get infected by a ___(a)___ called ___(b)___ which leads to a fatal blood disease called ___(c)___. Such risk faced by workers in any industry is called ___(d)___ ___(e)___.

Matching Type

1 Match the items given in column I with those given in column II:

Column I	Column II
(a) Selective breeding	(i) Washing of hair removed from sheep
(b) Rearing	(ii) Taking herds of sheep for grazing
(c) Shearing	(iii) Separating different textures
(d) Sorting	(iv) Removing fleece from sheep
(e) Scouring	(v) Selecting parents for obtaining special characters in their offspring

Very Short Answer Type Questions

1 How would you identify that the given fabric is made from new and pure wool?

2 Why do wool-yielding animals bear hair on their body?

3 How many types of fibres form sheep's hair?

4 Following are the steps involved in the processing of fibre into wool. Arrange them in a proper sequence:
Rearing, scouring, removing burr, shearing, sorting, making yarn, dyeing

Short Answer Type Questions

1 Why does a woollen garment keep us very warm in winter?

2 Observe the figures given below and name the various steps used in the process of making wool.

(a)

(b)

(c)

(d)

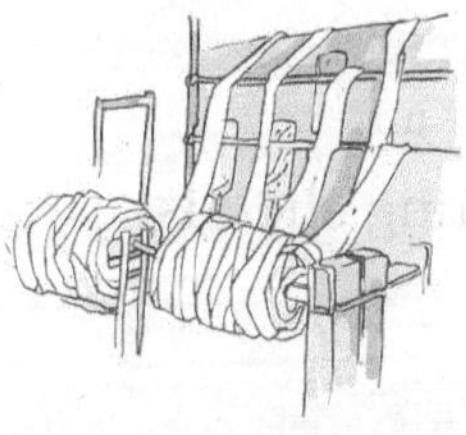

Long Answer Type Questions

1 (a) Is it fair to rear sheep and chop-off their skin for getting wool? Give reason for your answer.

(b) What is the basis to decide the quality of wool obtained from sheep?

Worksheet 2 Animal Fibre-Silk

Multiple Choice Questions (MCQs)

1 Rearing of silk worm to obtain silk is

(a) apiculture (b) sericulture

(c) scouring (d) shearing

2 Silk is widely used for making clothes.
Which one of the following gives raw silk?

(a) Big animals (b) Plants

(c) Insects (d) All of these

3 Which of the following stages in the life history of a silk produces silk fibres?

(a) 

(b) 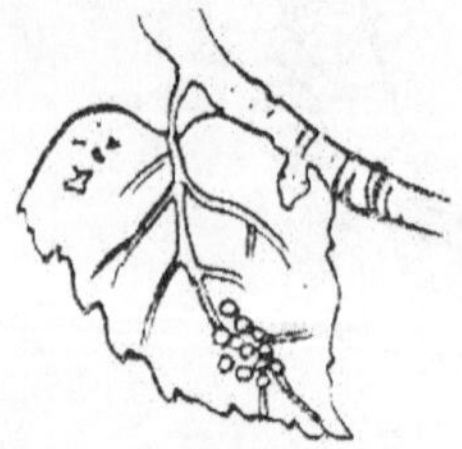

(c) 

(d) 

4 Which of the following is not a type of silk?

(a) Mulberry silk (b) Tassar silk

(c) Mooga silk (d) Moth silk

5 The general process that takes place at a sheep shearing shed is

(a) removal of fleece

(b) separating hair of different textures

(c) washing of sheep fibre to remove grease

(d) rolling of sheep fibre into yarn.

True/False

1 Write 'T' for True or 'F' for False for the following statements:

(a) Silkworms are caterpillars of silk moth. ☐

(b) Silk is obtained from the leaves of mulberry. ☐

(c) The scientific name of mulberry is *Morus alba*. ☐

(d) The most common silk moth is the mooga silk moth. ☐

(e) For reeling of silk, cocoons are boiled. ☐

Matching Type

1 Match the statements in column I with the words given in column II:

Column I (*Statement*)	Column II (*Word*)
(a) A variety of wild silk having a golden yellow colour	(i) Sericulture
(b) A pile of cocoons is used to obtain	(ii) China
(c) The science of rearing silk worms so as to obtain silk	(iii) Silk fibres
(d) The country which leads the world in silk production	(iv) Mooga
	(v) Japan

Fill in the Blanks

1 Fill in the blanks with the appropriate words:

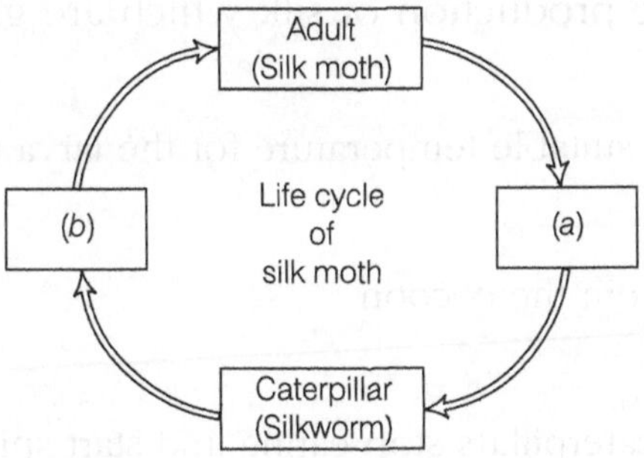

2 Fill in the blanks with the appropriate words given in the box:

good	*bad*	*protein*	*moth*	*sericulture*
cocoons	*minerals*	*pupa*	*reeling*	*warm*

(a) The process of taking out threads from the cocoons for use as silk is called ________ of the silk.

(b) Silk fibres are made of ________.

(c) Silk is obtained from ________.

(d) Silk cloth keeps us ________ as it is a ________ conductor of heat.

Give reasons for the following:

1 During the rearing of silkworms, the eggs are warmed to a suitable temperature.

2 Some cocoons are not boiled during harvesting of silk thread.

Very Short Answer Type Questions

1 Name the country where silk was first discovered.

2 Name the plant on which silk larva feeds.

3 Where does a female silk moth lay eggs?

4 What is pupa?

Short Answer Type Questions

1 Arrange the steps for the production of silk which are given below in a jumbled order.

(a) Eggs are warmed to a suitable temperature for the larva to hatch from eggs.

(b) Fibres are taken out from the cocoon.

(c) After 25-30 days, the caterpillars stop eating and start spinning cocoons.

(d) The larva/caterpillars or silkworms are kept in clean trays along with freshly chopped mulberry leaves.

(e) Female silk moths lay eggs.

(f) Cocoons are kept under the sun or boiled in water.

2 How are silk yarn of different textures prepared?

Long Answer Type Questions

1 How was silk discovered?

2 The following figure shows, for obtaining silk, moths are reared and their cocoons are collected to get silk threads. Study each diagram very carefully and answer the questions that follow.

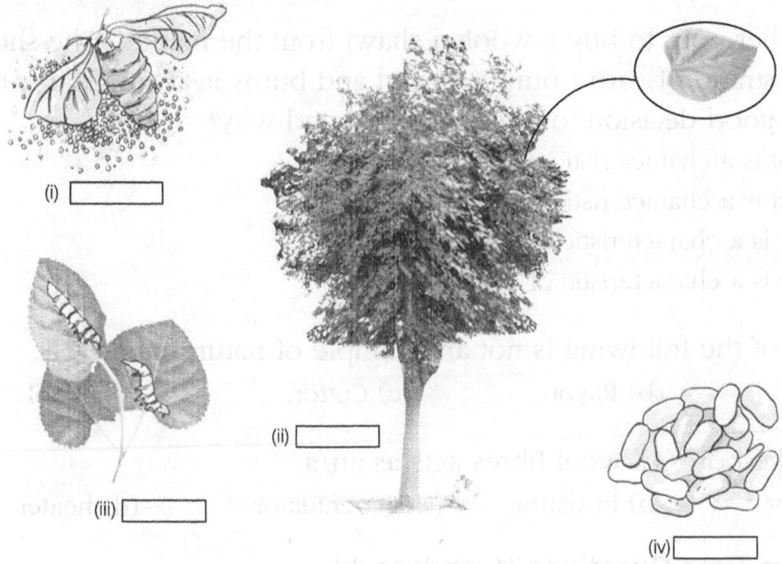

(a) Correctly fill the boxes (i), (ii), (iii) and (iv) to show the correct sequence.

(b) What is the use of mulberry tree?

(c) What treatment is given to the cocoons to separate out threads?

SUMMATIVE ASSESSMENT

BASED ON COMPLETE CHAPTER .....

Multiple Choice Questions (MCQs) (1 mark each)

1 The process of cleaning the fleece by using soap and a lot of water so as to remove dust, dirt and grease, etc. is called

(a) sorting (b) shearing

(c) washing (d) scouring

2 Silk and wool are

(a) protein fibres (b) carbohydrate fibres
(c) Both (a) and (b) (d) None of these

3 Nidhi's mother goes to buy a woolen shawl from the market. The shopkeeper takes out a small strand of yarn from the shawl and burns it. It smells like a burning plastic. Will it be a good decision to buy this shawl and why?

(a) Yes, as it is a characteristic of pure silk
(b) Yes, as it is a characteristic of pure wool
(c) No, as it is a characteristic of synthetic yarn
(d) No, as it is a characteristic of cotton

4 Which one of the following is not an example of natural fibre?

(a) Silk (b) Rayon (c) Cotton (d) Wool

5 The air in the pores of wool fibres acts as an/a

(a) conductor (b) insulator (c) ventilator (d) heater

Very Short Answer Type Questions (1 mark each)

1 What are burrs?

2 In which stage the silk moth spins the silk fibre around itself?

3 How many eggs can female silk moth lay?

4 Write atleast two characteristics of silk fibre.

5 Why are cocoons immersed in boiling water?

Short Answer Type I Questions (2 marks each)

1 What is meant by the term 'Reeling the silk'? How is it done?

2 What is meant by the 'rearing' and 'breeding' of sheep?

Short Answer Type II Questions (3 marks each)

1 Explain the food habits of sheep.

---

2 What kind of animals are reared in different regions for obtaining wool?

Long Answer Type Questions (5 marks each)

1 How silkworms are reared ? Explain.

---

2 Explain the phrase 'Unity is strength' on the basis of the making of fabric from fibre.

ACTIVITY (Word Search)

The given figure shows three rings of circle with letters in them. Some of these letters in each ring can form the name of one wool yielding animal. Find the names of these animals.

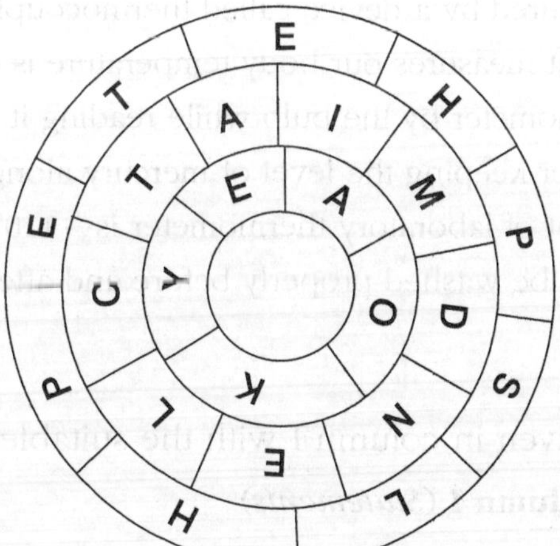

Chapter 4

Heat

Worksheet 1 Heat and Temperature

Fill in the Blanks

1 Fill in the blanks with the suitable words:

(a) Ensure that before use of clinical thermometer, the mercury level is below ________ °C.

(b) The normal temperature of human body is ________ °C. It may ________ person to person.

(c) The range of laboratory thermometer is ________ to ________.

(d) There is a ________ near the bulb of thermometer which prevents mercury level from falling on its own.

True/False

1 Write 'T' for True or 'F' for False for the following statements:

(a) Always rely your sense of touch to determine whether the object is hot or cold. ☐

(b) Temperature is measured by a device called thermocouple. ☐

(c) The thermometer that measures our body temperature is called a clinical thermometer. ☐

(d) Don't hold the thermometer by the bulb while reading it. ☐

(e) Read the thermometer keeping the level of mercury along any line of sight. ☐

(f) The lower fixed point of laboratory thermometer is – 110°C. ☐

(g) Thermometer should be washed properly before and after use. ☐

Matching Type

1 Match the statements given in column I with the suitable words given in column II:

Column I (*Statements*)	Column II (*Words*)
(a) A reliable measure of the hotness or coldness of an object	(i) 35°C
(b) Lower fixed point of clinical thermometer	(ii) 42°C
(c) Upper fixed point of clinical thermometer	(iii) Bimetallic thermometer
(d) A device which measures very high temperature	(iv) Temperature

Multiple Choice Questions (MCQs)

1 Which of the following is the most appropriate liquid for thermometric device?

(a) Water (b) Coloured water

(c) Alcohol (d) Mercury

2 Ram and Shyam measured their body temperature. Ram found it to be 98.6°F and Shyam recorded 37°C. Which of the following statement is correct?

(a) Ram has higher body temperature than Shyam

(b) Ram has lower body temperature than Shyam

(c) Both have normal body temperature

(d) Both are suffering from fever

3 Kritika has three thermometers as shown in figure. She wants to measure the temperature of her body and that of boiling water. Which thermometer(s) should she choose?

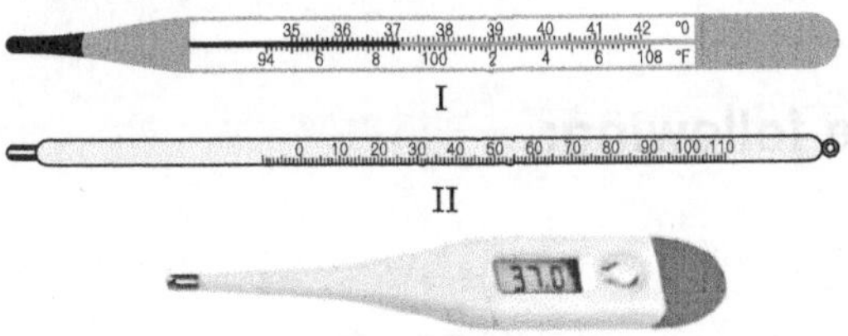

(a) Thermometer I or III for measuring body temperature and II for measuring the temperature of boiling water

(b) Thermometer I for measuring temperature of both

(c) Thermometer II for measuring temperature of both

(d) Thermometer III for measuring temperature of both

4 Figure (a-d) shows a student reading a doctor's thermometer. Which of the figure indicates the correct method of reading temperature?

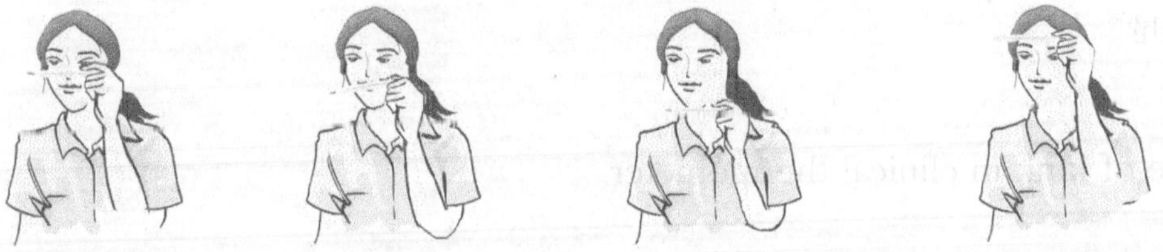

(a) (b) (c) (d)

5 Consider the statements and choose the correct option below:

I. Thermometer should be washed with antiseptic before and after use.

II. Before using thermometer, ensure that the mercury level is below 35°C.

(a) Only I (b) Only II

(c) Both I and II (d) None of these

Define the following terms:

1 Lower fixed point

2 Upper fixed point

Give reasons for the following:

1 A laboratory thermometer can't be used to measure temperature of a body.

2 Mercury is used in thermometer in place of water.

3 Always wash the thermometer with an antiseptic solution before and after use.

Differentiate between the following:

1 Heat and Temperature

2 Clinical and Laboratory thermometer

Very Short Answer Type Questions

1 What is the value of normal body temperature?

2 Why does the mercury not fall or rise in a clinical thermometer when taken in and out of the mouth?

3 Give the use of kink in clinical thermometer.

Short Answer Type Questions

1 You may have noticed that a few sharp jerks are given to clinical thermometer before using it. Why is it done so?

2 While taking measurement using laboratory thermometer it should be kept upright, not tilted. Why?

Long Answer Type Questions

1 List the precautions to be taken, while reading a clinical thermometer.

2 There are three large mugs in the figures *A*, *B* and *C*. Put cold water in mug *A* and hot water in mug *B*. Mix some cold and hot water in mug *C*. Now dip your right hand in mug *A* and left hand in mug *B*. After keeping the hands 2-3 minutes, put both the hands simultaneously in mug *C*. Do both the hands get the same feeling? Explain.

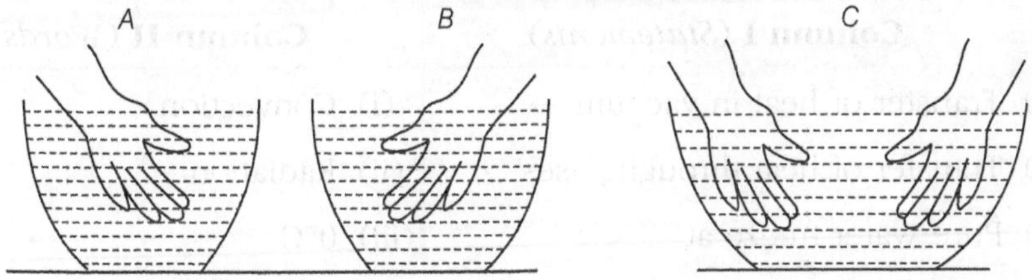

Worksheet 2 Transfer of Heat

Fill in the Blanks

1 Fill in the blanks with the suitable words:

(a) In solids, heat is transferred by the process of ________.

(b) The ________ and ________ are the poor conductors of heat.

(c) To receive cooler ________, the windows of the houses in coastal areas are made to face the sea.

(d) The cool air from the land moves towards the sea is called the ________.

(e) From the sun the heat comes to us by the process of ________.

(f) In summer, we should wear ________ coloured cloth whereas in winter ________ coloured cloth is preferred.

(g) When heat falls on some object, a part of it is ________ and a part is ________.

True/False

1 Write 'T' for True or 'F' for False for the following statements:

(a) A frying pan becomes hot when kept on flame due to convection. ☐

(b) Sea breeze is the movement of air from land to sea. ☐

(c) During the day, lands gets heated faster than water. ☐

(d) Radiation is the process of heat transfer which takes place easily in vacuum. ☐

(e) The transfer of heat through radiation don't require any medium. ☐

(f) A shining body can be considered as good absorber and good reflector. ☐

(g) The boiling point of pure water is 100°C . ☐

(h) A black surface is good radiator and bad absorber. ☐

(i) Dark coloured clothes absorbs more heat than light coloured clothes. ☐

Matching Type

1 Match the statements given in column I with the suitable words given in column II:

Column I (*Statements*)	**Column II** (*Words*)
(a) Transfer of heat in vacuum	(i) Convection
(b) Transfer of heat through gases	(ii) Radiation
(c) Pure water freeze at	(iii) 0°C
(d) Poor conductors of heat	(iv) Insulator

Multiple Choice Questions (MCQs)

1 When a heated pan is placed outside, it slowly cools down by the process of:

(a) Conduction (b) Convection

(c) Radiation (d) None of the above

2 Bulbs of wax are stuck to the wooden rod as shown in the figure. Which of these will melt first?

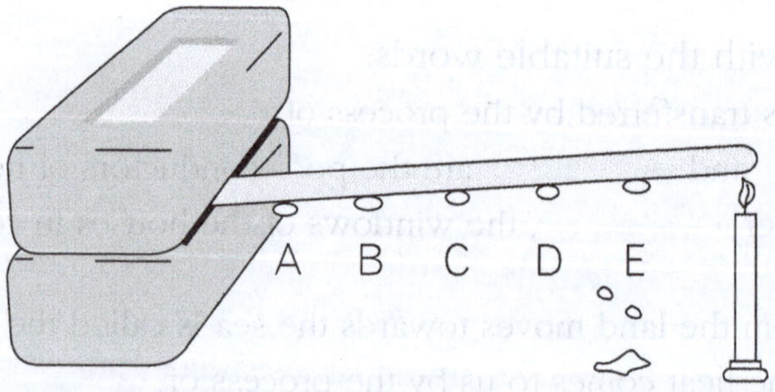

(a) *D* (b) *E*

(c) *A* (d) *B*

3 Sanjay has to carry cold coffee to his friend's home. Which of these will keep the coffee cold the longest?

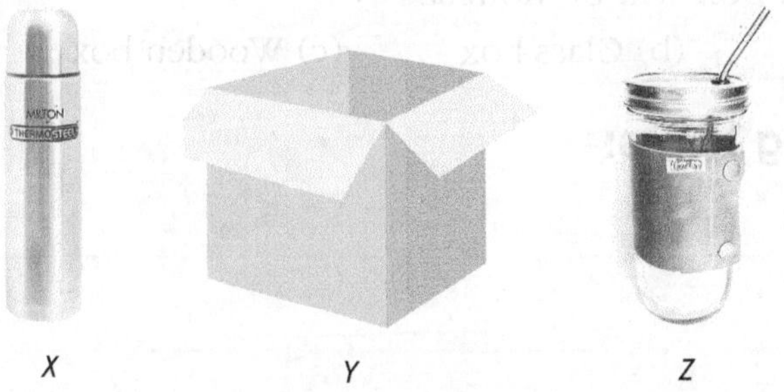

(a) *X* (b) *Y* (c) *Z* (d) None of these

4 Four boys went for a picnic on a hot days. Arjun wore a white shirt, Vikas wore a red shirt, Ankit wore a black shirt while Ajit wore a orange shirt. Who felt the heat most?

(a) Arjun, as white colour absorbs most heat (b) Ankit, as black colour absorbs most heat

(c) Vikas, as red colour absorb most heat (d) None of these

5 Sushmita wants to eat bread and jam. The lid of the jam bottle would not come off. Which of these will work best?

(a) Put it in a bucket of ice (b) Pour hot water over it

(c) Make a hole in the lid (d) Hammer it from all sides

6 A marble tile would feel cold as compared to a wooden tile on a winter morning, because the marble tile

(a) is a better conductor of heat than the wooden tile

(b) is polished while wooden tile is not polished

(c) reflects more heat than wooden tile

(d) is a poor conductor of heat than the wooden tile

7 Given diagram shows different processes of heat transfer.

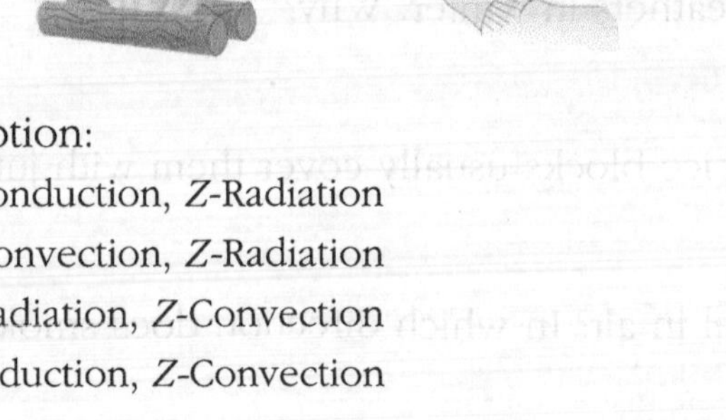

Choose the correct option:

(a) *X*-Convection, *Y*-Conduction, *Z*-Radiation

(b) *X*-Conduction, *Y*-Convection, *Z*-Radiation

(c) *X*-Conduction, *Y*-Radiation, *Z*-Convection

(d) *X*-Radiation, *Y*-Conduction, *Z*-Convection

8 Four boxes are left under the sun for half an hour. Boxes are made up of different material. Which box will be hottest?

(a) Iron box (b) Glass box (c) Wooden box (d) Plastic box

Define the following terms:

1 Radiation ______

2 Melting point ______

Give reasons for the following:

1 Convection is not possible in solids.

______

2 Handle of pressure cooker is covered with thick plastic.

______

3 Two thin clothes is more comfortable than a thick cloth in winter.

______

Differentiate between the following:

1 Conductor and Insulator

______

2 Conduction and Convection

______

Very Short Answer Type Questions

1 Choose odd one out and justify the correct choice:

(a) Wood, Iron, Steel, Copper

______

(b) Conduction, Radiation, Convection, Thermometer

______

2 Birds puff up their feathers in winter. Why?

______

3 Shopkeepers selling ice blocks usually cover them with jute sacks. Explain why?

______

4 How does heat travel in air? In which direction does smoke go?

______

Short Answer Type Questions

1 The water and air are the poor conductors of heat. Then, how does the heat transfer takes place in these substances?

2 Study the given figure carefully and answer the following questions:

(a) What can you observe from the above figures?

(b) What is the indication of these two figures?

3 Briefly explain why a mud house with the shed roofs keeps cool in summer?

Long Answer Type Questions

1 Water is being boiled in a pan of wide base. Observe the given figure carefully and answer the following questions:

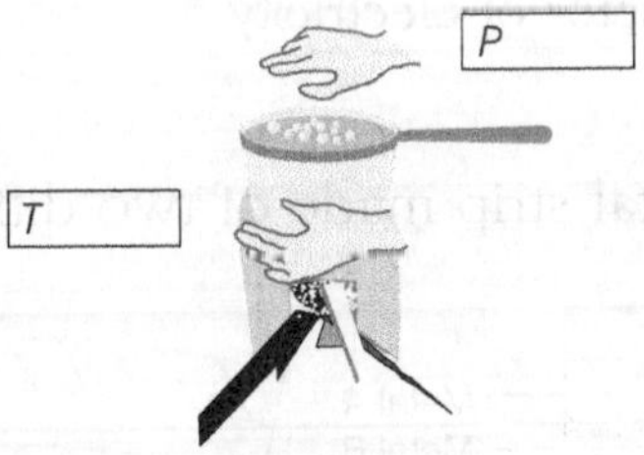

(a) Which position will feel warmer P or T?

(b) Fill up the boxes P and T to indicate the mode of flow of heat to the hand.

SUMMATIVE ASSESSMENT

BASED ON COMPLETE CHAPTER .....

Multiple Choice Questions (MCQs) (1 mark each)

1 Four arrangements to measure temperature of ice in beaker with laboratory thermometer are shown in figures (*a*, *b*, *c* and *d*). Which one of them shows the correct arrangement for accurate measurement of temperature?

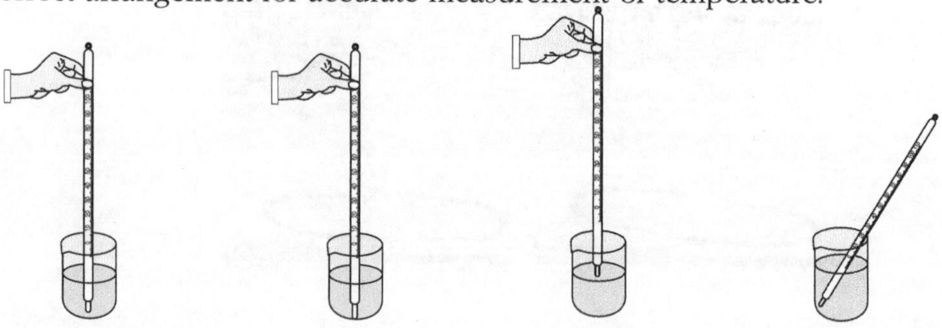

(a) (b) (c) (d)

2 The inner and outer surface of the flask is coated with plastic and steel. Why heat doesn't appear at the outer surface of the flask, if flask contains hot liquid?

(a) due to conduction between inner and outer surface

(b) due to insulation between inner and outer surface

(c) due to radiation between inner and outer surface

(d) due to convection between inner and outer surface

3 'Aluminium metal is used for making utensils for food preparation'. Which of the following option is correct regarding the above statements?

(a) Because it is a good conductor of heat

(b) Because it is a good insulator of heat

(c) Because it is a good conductor of electricity

(d) All of the above

4 Below diagram shows a metal strip made of two different metals *A* and *B*, before and after it had been heated.

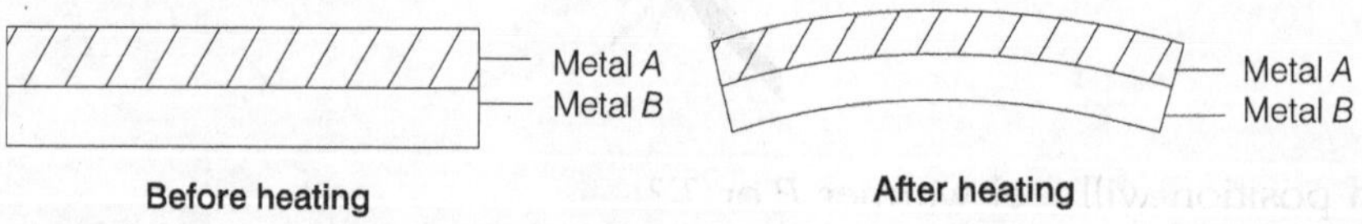

What can you infer from this experiment?

(a) Both metals don't expand

(b) Metal *A* expands more than metal *B*

(c) Metal *B* expands more than metal *A*

(d) None of the above

5 A beggar wrapped himself with a few layers of newspaper on a cold winter night. This helped him to keep himself warm because

(a) friction between the layers of newspaper produces heat

(b) air trapped between the layers of newspaper is a bad conductor of heat

(c) newspaper is a conductor of heat

(d) newspaper is at a higher temperature than the temperature of the surrounding

Very Short Answer Type Questions (1 mark each)

1 In a mercury thermometer, the level of mercury rises when its bulb comes in contact with a hot object. What is the reason for this rise in the level of mercury?

2 Study the diagram carefully and name the process by which transfer of heat is taking place.

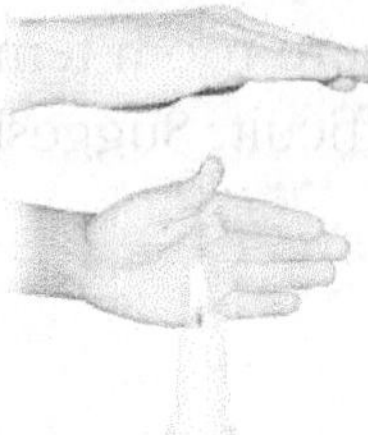

3 To keep her soup warm, Ritu wrapped the container in which it was kept with a woollen cloth. Can she apply the same method to keep a glass of cold drink cool? Give reason for your answer.

4 Name the liquid which is commonly used in making thermometer.

5 State the unit in which temperature is commonly measured

Short Answer Type I Questions (2 marks each)

1 Define conduction. Give one example where heat is transferred by the process of conduction.

2 Give the similarities and differences between the clinical thermometer and laboratory thermometer.

Short Answer Type II Questions (3 marks each)

1 One end of the objects such as a steel spoon, a plastic scale, a pencial and a divider is put in a beaker of hot water. In which of there objects the other end will get hot? Why?

---

2 Rahul found a begger was sleeping on the footpath on a winter night. He brought his thick blanket to give to that begger but his mother stopped him and gave him two thin blankets. Explain why?

Long Answer Type Questions (5 marks each)

1 For setting curd, a small amount of curd is added to warm milk. The microbes present in the curd help in setting if the temperature of the mixture remains approximately between 35°C-40°C. At places, where room temperature remains much below the range, setting of curd becomes difficult. Suggest a way to set curd in such a situation.

---

2 At a camp site, there are tents of two shades-one made with black fabric and the other with white fabric. Which one will you prefer for resting on a hot summer afternoon? Give reason for your choice. Would you like to prefer the same tent during winter?

ACTIVITY 1 (Crossword)

Complete the crossword with the help of clues given below:

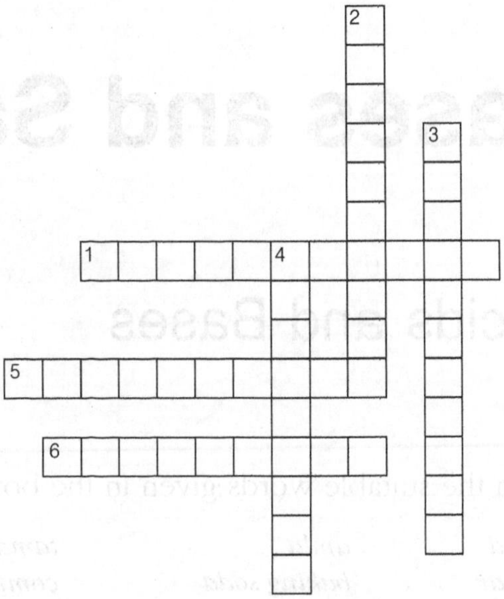

Across

1 Degree of hotness of an object.

5 In solid heat is transferred by this method.

6 These are also known as bad conductor of heat.

Down

2 Heat is transferred by this method in liquid and gas.

3 This device is used to measure temperature.

4 This method of transfer of heat doesn't require any medium.

ACTIVITY 2 (Word Identification)

Complete the following words:

(a) C _ _ _ _ C _ _ R

Hint: It allows heat to pass through it.

(b) C _ _ _ _ U _

Hint: This is a unit for measuring temperature.

(c) L _ _ _ _ R _ E _ _

Hint: The cool air moving towards the sea.

Chapter 5

Acids, Bases and Salts

Worksheet 1 Acids and Bases

Fill in the Blanks

1 Fill the flow chart with the suitable words given in the box:

lemon juice	*curd*	*amla*	*tamarind*
grapes	*sugar*	*baking soda*	*common salt*

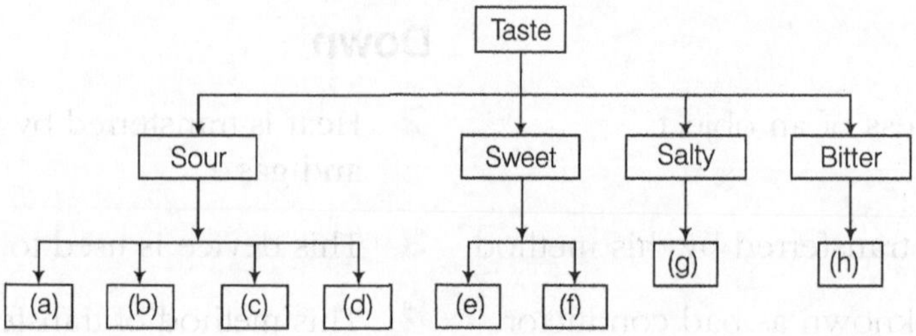

2 The following table shows the list of some naturally occurring weak acids. Complete the table with the appropriate words given in the box:

formic acid	*ascorbic acid*	*citric acid*	*curd*
vinegar	*spinach*	*grapes*	

	Name of acid	Found in
(i)	Acetic acid	_____(a)_____
(ii)	_____(b)_____	Ant's sting
(iii)	Oxalic acid	_____(c)_____
(iv)	Tartaric acid	_____(d)_____
(v)	_____(e)_____	Citrus fruits such as oranges, lemons, etc.
(vi)	Lactic acid	_____(f)_____
(vii)	_____(g)_____	Amla, citrus fruits

Multiple Choice Questions (MCQs)

1 What is the source of 'litmus' extraction?

(a) Lichen (b) Lime

(c) Litchi (d) None of these

2 Which of the following is an acid-base indicator?

(a) Turmeric (b) Vinegar (c) Baking soda (d) Lime water

3 Acid rain can cause damage to buildings, soil and plants. Where do you think the acid comes from?

(a) Calcium oxide and carbon dioxide dissolve in rain water to produce acid.

(b) Carbon dioxide and sulphur dioxide dissolve in rain water to produce acid.

(c) Sulphuric acid and carbon monoxide dissolve in rain water to produce acid.

(d) Chlorine and fluorine gases dissolve in rain water to produce acid.

4 Generally, pickles are not stored in tin vessels because

(a) tin is costly metal

(b) tin is denser metal

(c) tin is having high reactivity towards food components

(d) tin shows corrosive action

True/False

1 Write 'T' for True or 'F' for False for the following statements:

(a) Acids are bitter in taste. ☐

(b) Orange juice turns blue litmus red. ☐

(c) A compound of acidic nature will turn all indicators red. ☐

(d) Salt solution is basic in nature. ☐

(e) Generally all bases are soapy to touch. ☐

(f) Common salt dissolved in water turns blue litmus red. ☐

(g) Laboratory acids and bases are corrosive in nature. ☐

Matching Type

1 Match the bases in column I with their presence in column II:

Column I (*Base*)	Column II (*Found in*)
(a) Calcium hydroxide	(i) Milk of magnesia
(b) Magnesium hydroxide	(ii) Lime water
(c) Potassium hydroxide	(iii) Window cleaner
(d) Ammonium hydroxide	(iv) Soap

Give reasons for the following:

1 Acid cannot be stored in metal containers.

---

2 Baking soda does not taste sour.

---

3 When washed with soap, turmeric stain on a white shirt turns red.

---

4 While handling laboratory acids and bases, proper care should be taken.

Define the following terms:

1 Concentrated and dilute acids

---

2 Indicator

---

3 Acid rain

Short Answer Type Questions

1 Complete the following table:

Acid	Effect on litmus paper	Effect on turmeric paper	Effect on China rose solution
Lime water	red to blue	(a)	green
Sulphuric acid	blue to red	yellow	(b)
Sodium hydroxide	(c)	red	green
Dilute hydrochloric acid	blue to red	(d)	dark pink
Nitric acid	blue to red	yellow	(e)
Ammonium hydroxide	(f)	red	green
Acetic acid	blue to red	yellow	(g)

2 To make coloured water, dip some crushed China rose petals in warm water, add few drops of an acid and a base separately in two different containers. Write effect of acid and base on it.

Long Answer Type Questions

1 (a) While diluting an acid, the acid should be added to water and not water to the acid. Explain giving reason.

____

(b) Why should we take care while handling laboratory acids and bases?

____

2 You are provided with three test tubes *A*, *B* and *C* as shown in the figure below with different liquids. What will you observe when you put

(a) a piece of blue litmus paper in each test tube.

(b) a piece of red litmus paper in each test tube.

(c) a few drops of phenolphthalein solution to each test tube.

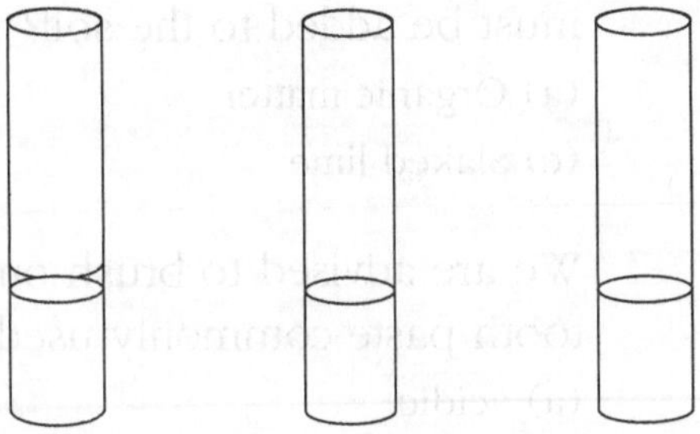

____

____

Worksheet 2 Neutralisation

Fill in the Blanks

1 Fill in the blanks with the appropriate words given in the box:

water	*slaked lime*	*heat*
salt	*hydrochloric acid*	*acidic*

(a) The products formed in a neutralisation reaction of an acid and a base are ________ and ________ with the evolution of ________.

(b) Our stomach contains ________.

(c) Calcium hydroxide is also known as ________.

(d) Excessive use of chemical fertilisers makes the soil ________.

True/False

1 Write 'T' for True or 'F' for False for the following statements:

(a) In a neutralisation reaction heat is always absorbed. ☐

(b) Sting of an ant contains vinegar. ☐

(c) Plants do not grow well when the soil is either too acidic or too basic. ☐

(d) Factory wastes should neutralised by adding neutral substances. ☐

Multiple Choice Questions (MCQs)

1 Phenolphthalein is a synthetic indicator and its colour in acidic and basic solutions, respectively are

(a) red and blue (b) blue and red

(c) pink and colourless (d) colourless and pink

2 When the soil is too basic, plants do not grow well in it. To improve its quality what must be added to the soil?

(a) Organic matter (b) Quick lime

(c) Slaked lime (d) Calamine solution

3 We are advised to brush our teeth regularly, to protect tooth decay. The nature of the tooth paste commonly used is

(a) acidic (b) basic

(c) neutral (d) corrosive

Very Short Answer Type Questions

1 Define the term 'neutralisation'.

2 Nidhi is suffering from indigestion due to acidity. Is it advisable to give her orange juice in this situation. Why/why not?

3 Name the natural acid found in ant's sting.

4 Name the chemical present in calamine solution.

Short Answer Type Questions

1 (a) Which acid is produced in our stomach?

(b) What happens if there is an excess of acid in the stomach?

(c) How can its effect be cured?

2 Explain why, calamine solution is applied on the skin when an ant bites?

Long Answer Type Questions

1 Radha observed that most of the fish in the pond of her village were gradually dying. She also observed that the waste of a factory in her village is flowing into the pond. What is the probable cause which led the fishes to die ?

(a) Explain why the fishes were dying?

____

____

(b) If the factory waste is acidic in nature, how can it be neutralised?

____

____

SUMMATIVE ASSESSMENT

BASED ON COMPLETE CHAPTER .....

Multiple Choice Questions (MCQs) (1 mark each)

1 Ramesh's teacher told him that acids are always stored in glass containers and not in metallic ones. Can you tell him why?

(a) Metals react with the acids stored in them

(b) We can see which acid it is through a glass bottle

(c) Glass containers are easily available

(d) Metal containers are expensive

2 Milk of magnesia is used as antacid because it is

(a) neutral (b) basic (c) acidic (d) None of these

3 The figures given below show the colour change in test tubes *A*, *B* and *C* when China rose indicator is added in them. The respective solutions in test tubes *A*, *B* and *C* are

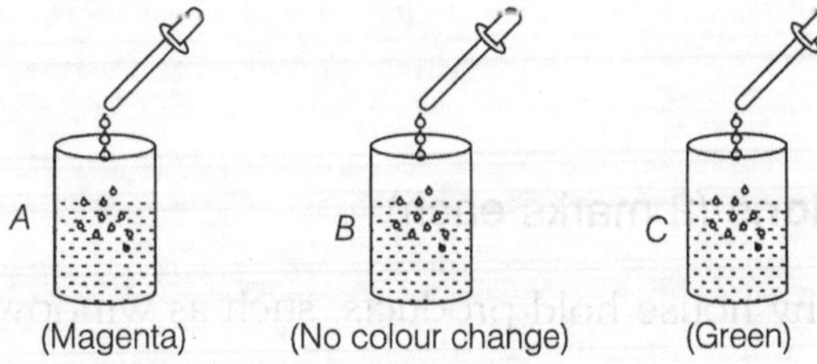

(a) sugar solution, lime water, baking powder

(b) lime juice, sugar solution, lime water

(c) lime water, sugar solution, lime juice

(d) sugar solution, lime juice, vinegar

4 Hydrochloric acid is the concentrated acid. Which one of the following organ secretes hydrochloric acid in the human body?

(a) Stomach

(b) Eyes

(c) Heart

(d) Ears

5 On adding phenolphthalein indicator to a colourless solution, no change is observed. What is the nature of this solution?

(a) Basic

(b) Either acidic or basic

(c) Either acidic or neutral

(d) Either basic or neutral

Very Short Answer Type Questions (1 mark each)

1 How many types of litmus paper are there?

____

2 A white shirt has a yellow stain of curry. When soap is rubbed on this shirt during washing, the yellow stain turns red. Name the natural indicator present in curry stain.

____

3 Complete the following reactions:

(a) $HCl + NaOH \rightarrow$ ______________________________

(b) $NaCl + H_2O \rightarrow$ ______________________________

4 Form a sentence using the following words baking soda, ant bite, moist, effect, neutralised, rubbing.

____

5 When an acid and a base solution are mixed in suitable amounts, what will be the resulting solution?

____

Short Answer Type I Questions (2 marks each)

1 Ammonia is found in many house hold products, such as window cleaners. It turns red litmus blue. What is its nature?

____

2 Is the distilled water acidic/basic/neutral? How would you verify it?

____

Short Answer Type II Questions (3 marks each)

1 Complete the following table:

Test solution	Effect on red litmus paper	Effect on blue litmus paper	Inference
Tap water	(a)	(b)	Neutral
Vinegar	(c)	Turns red	(d)
Washing soda	Turns blue	(e)	(f)

2 What is neutralisation reaction? Write an equation for neutralisation reaction. Is heat evolved or absorbed in a neutralisation reaction?

Long Answer Type Questions (5 marks each)

1 If we touch the test tube immediately after carrying out the neutralisation reaction of an acid and a base in it, it is found to be hot. Explain.

2 Why does soil in the field sometimes become highly acidic? Name two materials which can be added to this soil which reduces the acidity.

ACTIVITY 1 (Word Identification)

Fill in the blanks with appropriate word given in puzzle box:

1 Organic matter releases __1__ which neutralise the basic nature of the __2__. When the solution is __3__, phenolphthalein gives a __4__ colour.

B	A	S	I	C
O	C	O	L	O
P	I	N	K	Y
U	D	E	R	O
R	S	O	I	L

ACTIVITY 2 (Crossword)

Complete the crossword with the help of clues given below:

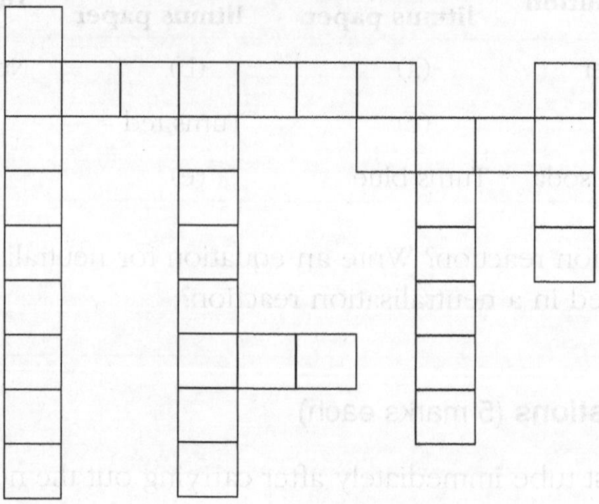

Across

2 The solution which does not change the colour of either red or blue litmus.

4 Phenolphthalein gives pink colour in this type of solution.

7 Colour of blue litmus in lemon juice.

Down

1 It is used to test whether a substance is acidic or basic.

3 It is a natural indicator and gives pink colour in basic solution.

5 Nature of ant's sting.

6 It is responsible for increase in temperature during a neutralisation reaction.

[Chapter 6]

Physical and Chemical Changes

True/False

1 Write 'T' for True or 'F' for False for the following statements:

(a) Tearing of a paper is a physical change. ☐

(b) Dissolving sugar in water is a chemical change. ☐

(c) Formation of clouds is a reversible change. ☐

(d) Hack-saw blade change colour on heating. ☐

(e) When a candle burns, both physical and chemical changes take place. ☐

(f) Stretching of rubber band is a physical change. ☐

(g) Melting of butter in a pan is a physical change. ☐

(h) It is not dangerous to look at the burning magnesium ribbon for a long time. ☐

(i) A man painted his main gate made up of iron, to make it look beautiful. ☐

(j) Iron benches kept in lawns and gardens get rusted. It is a physical change. ☐

Multiple Choice Questions (MCQs)

1 Which of the following are physical changes?

I. Melting of ice

II. Rusting of iron

III. Burning of iron filings

IV. Drawing a wire of iron metal

Choose the correct option:

(a) I and II (b) II and III

(c) I and IV (d) II and IV

2 Which will not acquire brown colour if left open after cutting?

(a) Apple (b) Onion

(c) Brinjal (d) Potato

3 Iron pillar near the Qutub Minar in Delhi is famous for the following facts. Which of these facts is responsible for its long stability?

(a) It is more than 7 metres high
(b) It weighs about 6000 kg
(c) It was built more than 1600 years ago
(d) It has not rusted after such a long period

4 The ozone layer in the upper atmosphere of Earth absorbs most of the

(a) ultrasonic radiations
(b) infrasonic radiations
(c) ultraviolet radiations
(d) infrared radiations

5 Fe (iron) + O_2(oxygen) + H_2O (water) → rust. The formula of rust is

(a) Fe_2O_3 (b) Fe_2O_4
(c) FeO (d) None of these

6 Which method is used to prevent rusting?

(a) Crystallisation (b) Galvanisation
(c) Sedimentation (d) None of these

7 Seema's mother made a concentrated sugar syrup by dissolving sugar in hot water. On cooling, crystals of sugar got separated. This indicates a

(a) physical change that can be reversed
(b) physical change that cannot be reversed
(c) chemical change that can be reversed
(d) chemical change that cannot be reversed

8 Which of the following among I, II and III represent a chemical change?

Growth of seed to a plant I

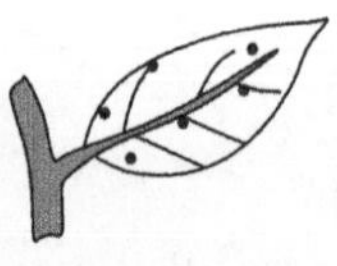

Formation of dew on leaves II

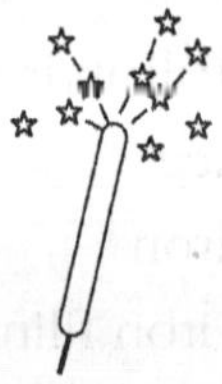

Burning of a sparkler III

(a) Both I and II
(b) Both II and III
(c) Both I and III
(d) All of the above

Fill in the Blanks

1 Fill in the blanks with the suitable words given in the box:

stainless steel	*chemical*	*water*
carbon dioxide	*oxygen*	*rusted*

(a) In the kitchen, a wet iron pan (tawa) often gets __________ if left in that state for some time.

(b) The lime water turns milky on passing __________ due to the formation of calcium carbonate.

(c) Photosynthesis and digestion of food are examples of __________ change.

(d) For rusting, the presence of both __________ and __________ is essential.

(e) __________ is made by mixing iron with carbon and metals like chromium, nickel and manganese.

(f) Ozone absorbs the ultraviolet radiation and breaks down to __________.

2 Select the physical and chemical changes and also shows the changes which are reversible by putting 'reverse' arrow in the following cases.

Process	Physical change	Chemical change
(a) Paper ⟶ Burnt paper		
(b) Cold water ⟶ Hot water		
(c) Raw mango ⟶ Ripe mango		
(d) Whole chalk ⟶ Broken chalk pieces		
(e) Ice ⟶ Water		
(f) Child ⟶ Adult		

Matching Type

1 Match the substances given in column I with their chemical formula given in column II:

Column I (*Substance*)	Column II (*Chemical formula*)
(a) Rust	(i) Calcium hydroxide, $Ca(OH)_2$
(b) Lime water	(ii) Ferric oxide, Fe_2O_3
(c) Blue vitriol	(iii) Calcium carbonate, $CaCO_3$
(d) Vinegar	(iv) Sodium hydrogencarbonate, $NaHCO_3$
(e) Baking soda	(v) Acetic acid, CH_3COOH
(f) Green vitriol	(vi) Calcium oxide, CaO
(g) Lime	(vii) Copper sulphate, $CuSO_4$
(h) Lime stone	(viii) Ferrous sulphate, $FeSO_4$

Define the following terms:

1 Galvanisation ______

2 Crystallisation ______

3 Ozone layer ______

4 Chemical reaction ______

Give reasons for the following:

1 Rusting of iron articles is faster in coastal areas than in deserts.

______

2 Setting of curd is regarded as a chemical change.

______

Very Short Answer Type Questions

1 Complete the following reactions:

(a) $\underset{\text{(Magnesium)}}{Mg} + \underset{\text{(Oxygen)}}{O_2} \longrightarrow$ ______

(b) $\underset{\text{(Magnesium oxide)}}{MgO} + \underset{\text{(Water)}}{H_2O} \longrightarrow$ ______

2 Write the chemical equation of the reaction occuring in the figure given below:

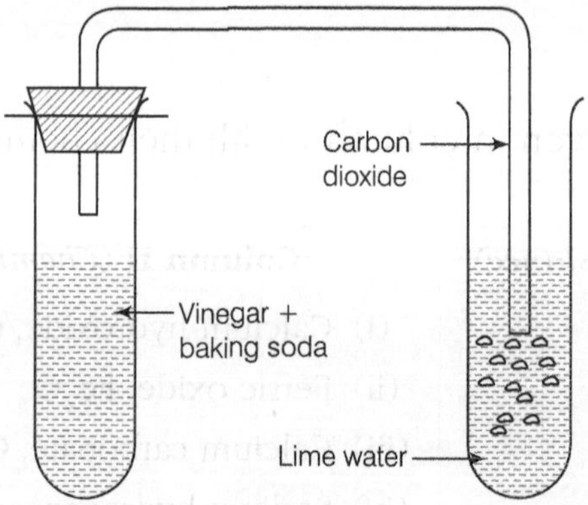

______

3 Why ships suffer a lot of damage from rusting inspite of being painted?

______

Short Answer Type Questions

1 Differentiate between Physical changes and Chemical changes.

2 *Step* I Two drops of dilute sulphuric acid were added to tea spoonful of copper sulphate powder and then small amount of hot water was added to dissolve it.
Step II On cooling, beautiful coloured crystals got separated.

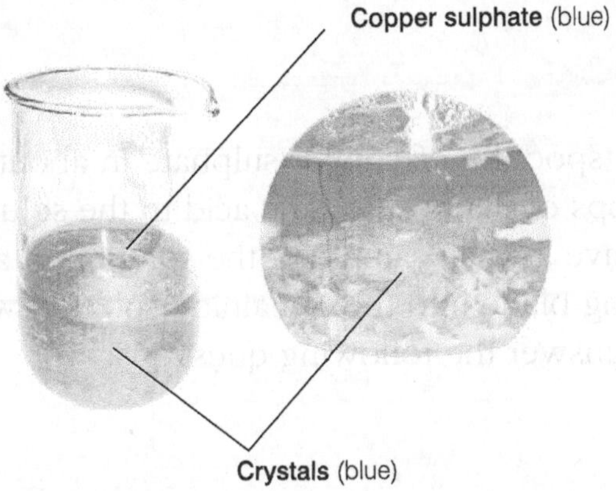

Identify the type of change in *step* I and *step* II, respectively.

3 What do you mean by rusting of iron? How it can be prevented?

Long Answer Type Questions

1 When magnesium is burned in air, a powdery ash '*A*' is formed, '*A*' on dissolving in water forms '*B*'.

(a) Identify (i) '*A*' and (ii) '*B*'.

(b) What is the action of '*B*' on litmus paper?

(c) What conclusion do you get about the nature of '*B*' from its action on litmus paper?

(d) Write the chemical equation of the reaction involved.

2 Dissolve about a tea spoonful of copper sulphate in about half a cup of water in a beaker. Add few drops of dilute sulphuric acid to the solution. You will get a blue coloured solution. Save a small sample of the solution in a test tube or a small glass bottle. Drop a shaving blade into the remaining solution wait for few hours. Based on this observation answer the following questions:

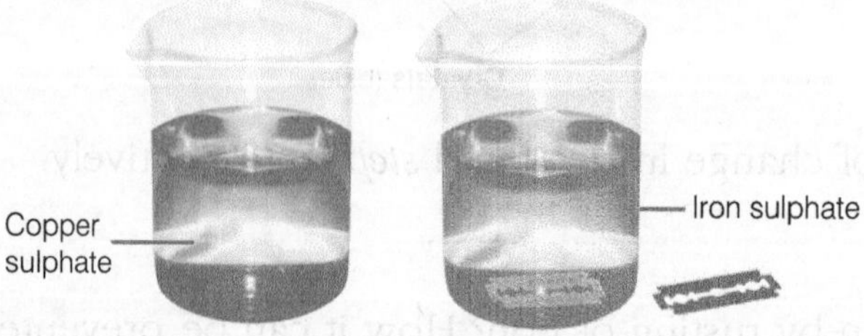

(a) What is the colour of copper and iron sulphate solutions?

(b) What is the colour of the blade after reaction?

(c) What change do you observe, when shaving blade dropped in copper sulphate solution?

(d) What type of change is this?

(e) Write the chemical equation of the reaction involved.

ACTIVITY 1 (Word Search)

Ozone absorbs …… and breakdown to oxygen. Ozone acts as a natural …… against radiation. Explosion of a fireworks is a kind …….. Burning of any substance is a …… change.

A	W	E	S	O	M	E	C	R	E
S	M	A	H	T	C	I	T	Y	A
R	A	D	I	A	T	I	O	N	R
A	C	H	E	M	I	C	A	L	N
D	P	O	L	L	U	T	I	O	N
I	O	L	D	E	S	K	T	O	P
A	O	C	T	I	C	A	T	I	O
T	I	T	A	N	I	C	N	O	L
E	M	E	R	G	E	N	C	Y	C
S	U	M	M	E	R	O	R	L	O

ACTIVITY 2 (Crossword)

Complete the crossword with the help of clues given below:

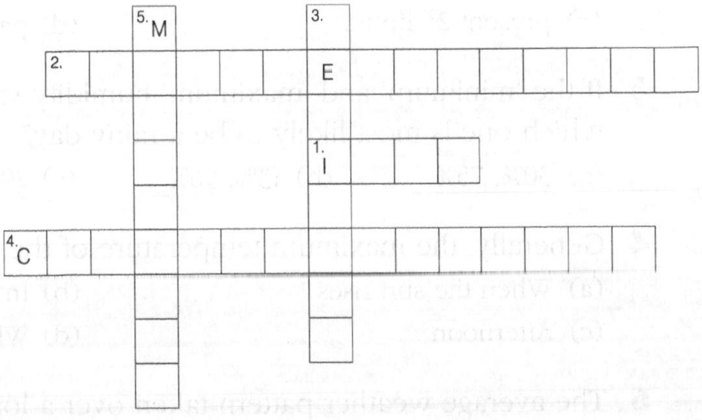

Across

1 It is used in making bridges, ships and cars.

2 Made by mixing iron with carbon and metals like chromium, nickel and manganese.

4 It is an example of a physical change.

Down

3 It is the end product of a chain of chemical reaction.

5 Magnesium oxide is formed on burning.

[Chapter 7]

Weather, Climate and Adaptations of Animals to Climate

Worksheet 1 Weather and Climate

Multiple Choice Questions (MCQs)

1 A person wants to make a daily weather report. Which of the following he/she is not likely to consider?

(a) Pressure (b) Temperature (c) Rainfall (d) Humidity

2 Weather report carries the information of

(a) day before yesterday (b) past 24 hours

(c) present 24 hours (d) past night

3 If the 'minimum' and 'maximum' humidity values on four different days are as given, which one is most likely to be a rainy day?

(a) 30%, 75% (b) 43%, 96% (c) 29%, 82% (d) 26%, 84%

4 Generally, the maximum temperature of the day occurs at what time of the day?

(a) When the sun rises (b) In mid noon

(c) Afternoon (d) When the sunsets

5 The average weather pattern taken over a long time is called the climate of the place. Here, long time means about

(a) 5 years (b) 10 years (c) 25 years (d) 3 years

6 Read the data mentioned below carefully:

I. It has extremes of temperature during day and night.

II. It has little rainfall. III. It is extremely hot and dry.

Which state is characterised by it?

(a) Kerala (b) Jammu and Kashmir

(c) Uttar Pradesh (d) Rajasthan

Fill in the Blanks

1 Fill in the blanks with the suitable words:

(a) The Meteorology department of the government makes __________ reports daily.

(b) The days are __________ in summer than in winter.

(c) __________ temperature of the day is usually recorded in the early morning.

(d) __________ is never constant at a place.

(e) The Sun is a huge sphere of __________ gases at a very __________ temperature.

True/False

1 Write 'T' for True or 'F' for False for the following statements:

(a) Prediction of weather in advance is called as weather forecasting ☐

(b) The time of sunrise and sunset changes during the year. ☐

(c) If the amount of moisture in the air is low, we say that the humidity is high. ☐

(d) Climate at a place may change suddenly. ☐

(e) It is easy to predict weather rather than climate. ☐

(f) In Rajasthan, typical desert climate is found. ☐

Matching Type

1 Match the following places or regions of India in column I with their respective climate in column II:

Column I (*Regions*)	Column II (*Climate*)
(a) Mumbai	(i) Very hot summers and cold winters
(b) Kerala	(ii) Very cold
(c) Himalayas	(iii) High humidity
(d) Delhi	(iv) Neither too cold nor too hot
(e) Rajasthan	(v) Low humidity

Answer the following statements in one word:

1 The measure of moisture in the air.

____

2 An instrument used to measure rainfall.

____

3 The unit in which rainfall is measured.

____

4 An instrument used to measure temperature.

____

5 The unit in which temperature is measured.

Differentiate between the following:

1 Humidity and Rainfall

2 Maximum and Minimum temperatures of a day

Define the following terms:

1 Humidity

2 Weather

3 Climate

Very Short Answer Type Questions

1 Name the elements of weather.

2 What is the main cause of changes in weather?

3 The temperature of a place is high most of the time and there is heavy rainfall on most of the days. What type of climate does this place have?

Short Answer Type Questions

1 Why is it difficult to predict the weather of a place while it is easy to predict its climate?

2 In summer, we feel miserable in the afternoon and comparatively comfortable in the early morning. Explain the cause.

Long Answer Type Questions

1 State and explain the factors on which climate of a region depends.

2 How does the Sun decide the weather at any place?

3 How can you find out mean temperature of a month? Give example.

Worksheet 2 Adaptations of Animals

True/False

1 Write 'T' for True or 'F' for False for the following statements:

(a) Since, very few prey are available, polar bear does not need to have strong sense of smell. ☐

(b) A layer of fat under skin in polar bears is an adaptation against extremely hot climate. ☐

(c) Penguins stick together to fight the cold polar climate. ☐

(d) Tropical rainforests are cool and humid throughout the year because of heavy rain all the time. ☐

Multiple Choice Questions (MCQs)

1 A tropical rainforest is not likely to be present in a country such as

(a) India (b) Brazil (c) Malaysia (d) Canada

2 Penguins keep their body warm by

(a) flapping their wings (b) moving around constantly

(c) hibernating in winters (d) huddling together

3 Beard ape rarely comes down on the ground because

(a) it cannot walk (b) it is easily attacked by predators

(c) it is a good climber (d) it gets sufficient food on the trees

4 Rahul went to a wildlife sanctuary where he saw dense vegetation of trees, shrubs, herbs and a variety of animals like monkeys, birds, elephants, snakes, frogs, etc. The most likely location of this sanctuary is in the

(a) temperate region (b) tropical region
(c) polar region (d) coastal region

5 Elephants living in tropical rainforest adapt themselves to their climate by the following adaptations except

(a) large fan like ears (b) tusks
(c) large pillar like legs (d) streamlined body

Matching Type

1 Match the following animals in column I with their characteristics in column II:

Column I (*Animal*)	**Column II** (*Characteristic*)
(a) Red eyed frog	(i) Sensitive hearing
(b) Penguin	(ii) Streamlined body
(c) Tiger	(iii) Silver-white mane
(d) Lion-tailed macaque	(iv) Sticky pads on feet
(e) New world monkey	(v) Long tail

Define the following terms:

1 Big cats ______

2 Camouflage ______

3 Equator ______

Give 3-4 examples of each of the following:

1 Regions of tropical rainforest.

______

2 Countries belonging to polar region.

______

3 Animals living in tropical rainforests.

______

4 Animals living in polar regions.

______

5 Animals which can camouflage.

______

Give reasons for the following:

1 Lion-tailed macaques live in Western Ghats.

2 Toucans have large beaks.

3 Birds never get lost while travelling.

4 Elephants have long ears.

5 Monkeys have long tails.

Differentiate between the following:

1 Climate of polar region and Climate of tropical rainforest

2 Migration and Adaptation

3 Webbed feet and Sticky pads on feet

Very Short Answer Type Questions

1 What determines the types of animals found in different parts of the world?

2 The bird *X* moves from Siberia to places like Rajasthan and Haryana in India during a particular season. It stays in India for a few months and then goes back.

(a) Name the bird *X*.

(b) What general name is given to birds like *X*?

(c) Name the season during which bird *X* moves from Siberia to India.

Short Answer Type Questions

1 Why is the colour of polar bear white?

2 Why do birds migrate?

3 What are tusks in elephants? How does an elephant use them?

Long Answer Type Questions

1 How do the following animals adapt their body to survive in the polar region?

(a) Polar bear

(b) Penguin

2 What are the various adaptations of animals living in tropical rainforest? Explain with examples.

SUMMATIVE ASSESSMENT

BASED ON COMPLETE CHAPTER .....

Multiple Choice Questions (MCQs) (1 mark each)

1 The maximum and minimum temperature displayed daily in the weather bulletin refer to the

(a) highest day temperature and lowest night temperature of the day
(b) highest day temperature and highest night temperature of the month
(c) temperature recorded at 12 noon and at mid night (00.00 hrs)
(d) average highest temperature of day and average lowest temperature of night

2 Read the following environmental conditions of tropical rainforests.

I. Hot and humid climate
II. Unequal lengths of day and night
III. Abundant rainfall
IV. Abundant light and moisture

Identify the conditions from the above list that are responsible for the presence of large number of plants and animals in tropical rainforests.

(a) Both I and II (b) Both I and III (c) I, III and IV (d) Both II and IV

3 Study the graph and answer the following question:
The average temperature during the week is

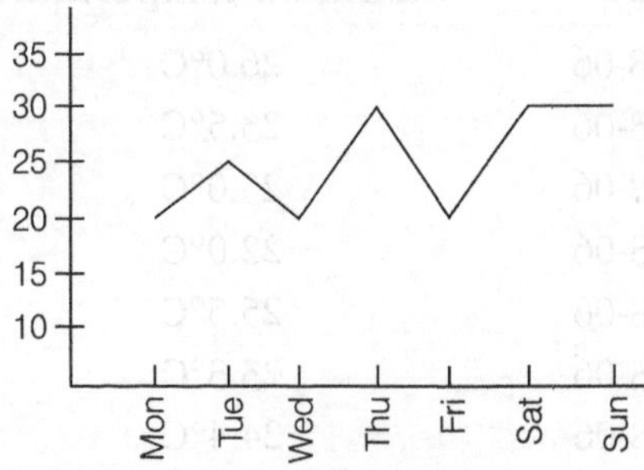

(a) 30°C (b) 25°C (c) 32°C (d) 20°C

4 Given below are the adaptations of polar bear. Which of the following are not meant for hunting prey and getting protection from predators?

I. White colour of the fur
II. Strong sense of smell
III. Long hair between the pads on its feet
IV. Two thick layers of the fur
V. Sharp claws on each foot

Choose the correct option:

(a) Both I and V (b) Both III and IV (c) Both II and III (d) Both I and IV

5 The short-term variation which occurs in the atmosphere is called

(a) climate (b) humidity (c) climate chart (d) weather

Very Short Answer Type Questions (1 mark each)

1 Name two places in India where Siberian crane migrates during winters.

2 Name two regions of the earth with extreme climatic conditions.

3 What is the most outstanding feature of lion-tailed macaque?

4 What is the difference between climate of Kashmir and Kerala?

5 Write the names of two animals which live in Indian tropical rainforests.

Short Answer Type I Questions (2 marks each)

1 State the information that can be drawn from a daily weather report.

2 Given below is a table showing the maximum temperature from 3-08-06 to 9-08-06:

Date	Maximum temperature
03-08-06	26.0°C
04-08-06	23.5°C
05-08-06	25.0°C
06-08-06	22.0°C
07-08-06	25.5°C
08-08-06	23.3°C
09-08-06	24.4°C

(a) Draw a graph from the data given in the table.

(b) What conclusion can be drawn from the graph?

Short Answer Type II Questions (3 marks each)

1 (a) How has a toucan adapted itself to the competition for food that exists in the rainforests?

(b) What purpose do the large ears of the elephant serve?

2 How do birds find direction when they migrate? Give atleast three ways.

Long Answer Type Questions (5 marks each)

1 Given below is a table showing different animals. Fill in the table with any one climatic adaptation of that animal with the usefulness of that adaptation.

	Animal	Adaptation	Usefulness		Animal	Adaptation	Usefulness
(a)		I	(i)	(d)		IV	(iv)
(b)		II	(ii)	(e)		V	(v)
(c)		III	(iii)				

2 (a) Weather may have a profound effect on our daily activities. Justify with examples.

(b) Why do many tropical animals have sensitive hearing, thick skin and skin colour? Also, give few examples of such animals.

ACTIVITY 1 (Jumbled Word)

Unscramble the following words using the hints given below:

(a) Weather pattern in a region over a period of time.
MATLICE

(b) Coolest region on earth.
AROPL

(c) Used to measure temperature.
TREHMEOMRET

(d) Feature of weather.
UHIDYTMI

ACTIVITY 2 (Word Matching)

Given below is a list of climatic conditions and some examples of animals. Read them carefully and place the items in the relevant columns as shown.

Penguin, Gorilla, Monkey, Reindeer, Assam, Greenland, Sun does not rise for six months, Hot and humid climate, Days and nights are almost equal in length throughout the year, Winter temperature around –37°C, Western Ghats

Tropical rain forest	Polar region
• Hot and Humid Climate	• Penguin

Chapter 8

Winds, Storms and Cyclones

Worksheet 1 Winds

Fill in the Blanks

1 Fill in the blanks with the suitable words:

(a) Increased wind speed is accompanied by __________ air pressure.

(b) The warm air is __________ than cold air.

(c) The main cause of wind movement is uneven __________ on the earth.

(d) In winter, the direction of flow of __________ reverses and it flows from __________ to the __________.

True/False

1 Write 'T' for True or 'F' for False for the following statements:

(a) Air moves from low pressure region towards the high pressure region. ☐

(b) Regions close to the equator get maximum heat from the Sun. ☐

(c) At the poles, the air is colder than that at latitudes about 60 degrees. ☐

(d) Uneven heating of land and water in winter generate winds from the North-West colder land. ☐

(e) Uneven heating of land generates monsoon winds from South-West direction in summer. ☐

Multiple Choice Questions (MCQs)

1 On blowing air into balloon, the size of the balloon increases, because

(a) warm air rises up

(b) air exerts pressure

(c) air is stronger than balloon

(d) None of the above

2 A curtain is hanging at the entrance of a room. A long corridor runs at right angles to the door, that is parallel to the curtain. If a strong wind blows along the corridor, the curtain will

(a) get pushed inside the room (b) get pushed outside the room
(c) get collected towards one end/swirled (d) remain unaffected

3 In winter, which wind blow from the ocean to the land?

(a) Winter (b) Summer (c) Autumnal (d) Monsoon

Matching Type

1 Match the words given in column I with the suitable words given in column II:

Column I	Column II
(a) Wind	(i) Winds carrying water
(b) Monsoon	(ii) Contracts
(c) On heating, air	(iii) Moving air
(d) On cooling, air	(iv) Expands

Very Short Answer Type Questions

1 Which factor is responsible for the increase of speed of wind?

2 Why leaves of trees, banners or flag flutter when the wind is blowing?

3 It is difficult to ride a bicycle against the direction of wind. Explain.

4 To expel hot air out of the kitchen, '*A*' has an exhaust fan fitted on the window of her kitchen and '*B*' has a similar exhaust fan fitted on the wall near the ceiling of her kitchen. Which of the exhaust fan will expel the hot air more effectively? Why?

Short Answer Type Questions

1 Consider the diagram given below and answer the following questions:

(a) When strong/high speed wind blows, an umbrella held upright at time sets upturned. Why?

(b) What does the above figure shows?

(i) (ii)

2 Observe the diagrams given below and answer the following questions:

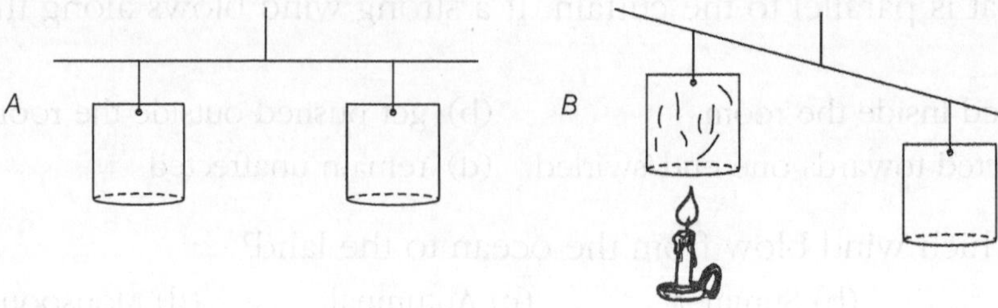

(a) Explain the result observed by this activity.

(b) Why smoke always rises up?

Long Answer Type Questions

1 When cold water is poured over a tin can full of steam and corked tightly, the tin can gets crushed. (as shown in the figure)

(a) What does the above activity indicates?

(b) What else can be taken instead of tin can? How can the activity be performed with that?

2 Explain the following observation:

When we blow over a paper strip it goes upward (as shown in the given figure below).

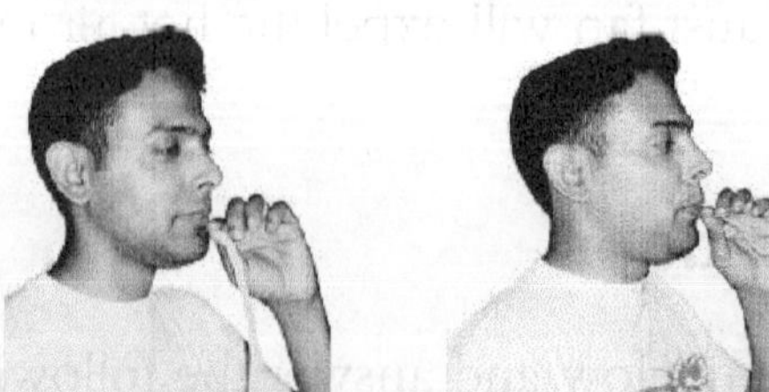

Does this process responsible for lifting of weak roof. When high-speed winds blew over them? How?

Worksheet 2 Thunderstorms and Cyclones

Very Short Answer Type Questions

1 What is meant by the term "Thunderstorm"?

2 What is an eye of the cyclone?

3 What is a cyclone known as in

(a) American continent?

(b) Phillippines and Japan?

4 Which one is more frequent in India, cyclones or tornadoes?

5 What is the difference between cyclone alert or cyclone warning?

True/False

1 Write 'T' for True or 'F' for False for the following statements:

(a) Thunderstorm is only associated with heavy rainfall. ☐

(b) Thunderstorms develop in hot, humid tropical areas like India very frequently. ☐

(c) A very high pressure system, surrounded with very high speed wind forms a cyclone. ☐

(d) The coast line of India is not vulnerable to cyclones. ☐

(e) A tornado shelter is a room situated deep inside having lots of windows. ☐

(f) A violent tornado can travel at speed of about 300 km/h. ☐

Short Answer Type Questions

1 Write (Yes/No) against the precautions you should follow when storm is accompanied by lightning:

Precautions	Yes/No
Do not take shelter under an isolated tree	
Lie on the ground	
Do not take shelter under an umbrella with a metallic end	
Sit near a window	
Open garages, storage sheds, metal sheds are not safe places to take shelter	
If you are in water, get out and go inside a building	
A car or a bus is not a safe place to take shelters	

2 How does the thunderstorm become cyclone?

Matching Type

1 Match the words given in column I with the suitable words given in column II:

Column I	Column II
(a) Dark funnel shaped cloud	(i) Indication of approaching cyclone
(b) Satellites	(ii) Tornado
(c) Water-wall	(iii) Diameter of the eyes
(d) 10-30 km	(iv) Track cylones

Define the following terms:

1 Cyclone

2 Tornadoes

Multiple Choice Questions (MCQs)

1 Which of the following place is most likely to be affected by a cyclone?
(a) Puri (b) Mumbai (c) Porbandar (d) Goa

2 The instrument which is used to measure the speed of the wind is
(a) speedometer (b) barometer
(c) anemometer (d) agorometer

3 During a cyclones, why is it difficult for meteorologist to forecast, what will happen?

(a) As cyclones can change direction suddenly

(b) As cyclones are very violent

(c) Because they do not have instruments to judge cyclones

(d) None of the above

4 Identify the given storm:

(a) Hurricane (b) Cyclone (c) Typhoon (d) Tornado

Long Answer Type Questions

1 Why are cyclones so destructive? Describe how a cyclone causes widespread destruction leading to a great loss of life and property?

2 Explain in detail, the disaster management of a cyclone.

SUMMATIVE ASSESSMENT

BASED ON COMPLETE CHAPTER .....

Multiple Choice Questions (MCQs) (1 mark each)

1 Which of the following is the first indication of an approaching cyclone?

(a) Powerful water waves (b) Cool breeze and rains

(c) Rains accompanied by lighting (d) None of these

2 A fire alarm usually detects smoke in case of fire. Where should such an alarm be placed in a room?

(a) Near the door (b) On the floor (c) On any wall (d) On the ceiling

3 What lifts the water surface in the centre of the cyclone?

(a) Low pressure in the eye of the cyclone

(b) Low pressure of arising winds

(c) High pressure in the eye of the cyclone

(d) High pressure of arising winds

4 Which of these are effective safety measures with regard to a cyclone?

I. A cyclone forecast and warning service.

II. Arrangement to move people quickly to safer areas.

III. Rapid communication with all people.

Choose the correct option:

(a) Only I (b) Both I and III (c) I, II and III (d) Only III

5 A violent storm lifts people and cars off the ground and hurls them hundreds of metres away. This storm is likely to be a

(a) thunderstorms (b) tornado (c) cyclone (d) typhoon

Very Short Answer Type Questions (1 mark each)

1 The diagram given below represents trees in the afternoon along a sea coast. State on which side is the sea; *A* or *B*? Give reasons for your choice.

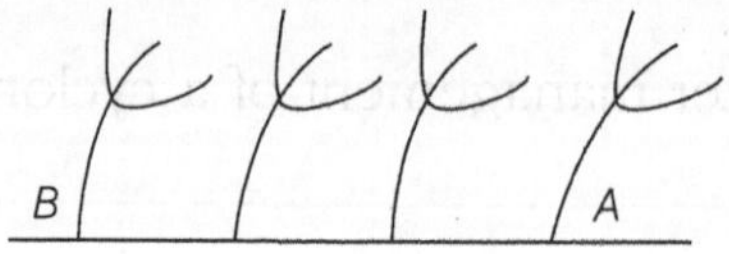

____

2 At what speed wind becomes a gentle breeze and a storm?

____

3 When you drink a cold drink with a straw, what forces the liquid to rise up in the straw?

____

4 Name the two technologies which help in making a forecast of a cyclone.

____

5 Write the full form of NSSL.

____

Short Answer Type I Questions (2 marks each)

1 How does lightning occur during a storm?

2 Bicycle tubes burst when they are overfilled. Why?

Short Answer Type II Questions (3 marks each)

1 A flat in Mumbai with a balcony facing the sea has some clothes hung on a clothes line in the balcony. Towards which direction, the clothes will be blown in the afternoon? Explain.

2 Due to uneven heating of 'land' and ocean water:

(a) In which season do winds blow from land towards ocean?

(b) In which season do winds blow from ocean towards land?

Long Answer Type Questions (5 marks each)

1 A paper kept at the mouth of a bottle doesn't go inside if we blow air on the mouth of the bottle as shown in the figure. Give reason.

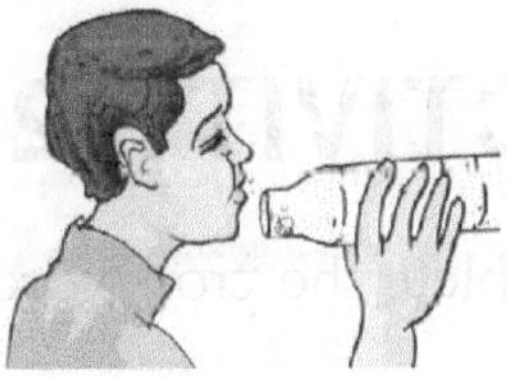

2 When we blow air in the space between two inflated balloons (carrying a little water each) and hanging about 10 cm apart on a stick, the two balloons come closer. Explain.

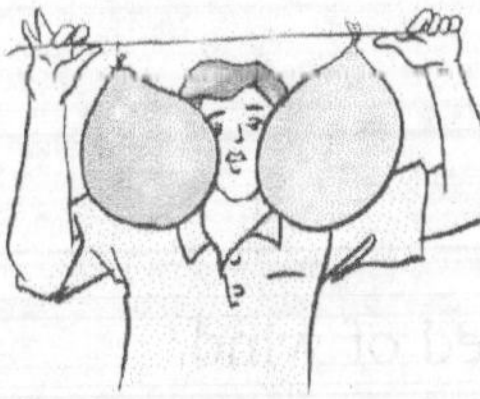

ACTIVITY 1 (Word Search)

1 Identify the names of six natural phenomena from the following word diagram:

G	C	H	T	H	T	E	N	M	R
R	C	Y	H	O	O	N	C	Z	P
V	L	O	U	E	R	O	E	R	T
A	N	C	N	A	N	N	L	C	L
H	T	H	D	B	A	D	A	P	I
L	U	N	E	K	D	C	Y	D	G
H	U	R	R	I	C	A	N	E	H
W	C	T	S	L	M	N	O	P	T
M	Y	O	T	Y	P	H	O	O	N
O	C	R	O	H	C	T	P	Q	I
C	L	N	R	U	A	Y	R	S	N
F	O	A	M	R	N	P	T	U	G
P	N	D	X	R	E	H	Y	E	N
Z	E	O	A	I	O	U	N	Y	B

ACTIVITY 2 (Crossword)

Complete the crossword with the help of clues given below:

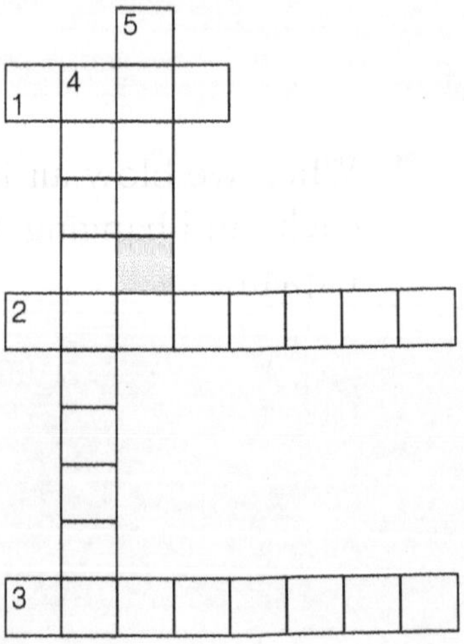

Across

1 This is brought by winds carrying water vapour.

2 Air expands on heating and ______ on cooling.

3 Air around us exerts ______ .

Down

4 This is used to measure the speed of wind.

5 This is the moving air.

[Chapter 9]

Soil

Worksheet 1 Soil: Profile and its Types

True/False

1 Write 'T' for True or 'F' for False for the following statements:

(a) Waste products and chemicals should be treated before they are released into the soil. ☐

(b) A-horizon provides shelter for many living organisms. ☐

(c) B-horizon is made up of small lumps of rocks with crack and crevices. ☐

(d) The mixture of rock particles and humus is called clay. ☐

(e) The best topsoil for growing plants is clayey soil. ☐

(f) Silt makes the soil fertile and provides nutrients to the growing plants. ☐

Fill in the Blanks

1 Fill in the blanks with the suitable word given in the brackets:

(a) When we talk of soil, it actually means ________. (bedrock/topsoil)

(b) The roots of small plants are embedded entirely in the ________. (A-horizon/B-horizon)

(c) B-horizon has a ________ amount of humus, but ________ minerals. (lesser/more)

(d) Middle layer of the soil has ________ amount of humus. (more/less)

(e) ________ is hard and difficult to dig with a spade. (C-horizon/Bedrock)

(f) If the amount of large and fine particles is ________, then the soil is loamy soil. (same/different)

(g) The smallest rock particles present in the soil form ________. (clay/silt)

Multiple Choice Questions (MCQs)

1 Availability of water and minerals in the soil for maximum absorption by roots is in the

(a) B-horizon (b) C-horizon

(c) A-horizon (d) surface of the soil

2 Which of the following shows the composition of soil containing rock particles?
(a) Air + water
(b) Water + plants
(c) Minerals + organic matter + air + water
(d) Water + air + plants

3 Soil has particles of different sizes. Which of the following option shows the correct increasing order of these particles?
(a) Rock < Clay < Sand < Gravel < Silt
(b) Rock < Sand < Clay < Silt < Gravel
(c) Clay < Sand < Silt < Rock < Gravel
(d) Clay < Silt < Sand < Gravel < Rock

4 For making the soil fertile, we should mix which of the following with tiny rock particles?
(a) Clay (b) Silt (c) Humus (d) Sand

5 Soil pollution cannot be caused by
I. Jute bag II. Acid rain
III. Cardboard IV. Plastic bag
Choose the correct option.
(a) I and II (b) II and III (c) I and III (d) III and IV

Matching Type

1 Match the animals in column I with their natural place of dwelling (habitat) in column II:

Column I (*Animals*)	Column II (*Habitat*)
(a) Earthworm	(i) Sand and beaches
(b) Garden lizard	(ii) Burrows in soil
(c) Crab	(iii) Deep, narrow holes in dry soils
(d) Rodents	(iv) Surface of the soil
(e) Scorpion	(v) Surface of shaded moist soils
(f) Snails and slugs	(vi) A-horizon of moist soils

Define the following terms:

1 Natural resources ____________

2 Humus ____________

3 Weathering ____________

4 Soil profile ______

5 Bedrock ______

6 Soil ______

7 Silt ______

Give reasons for the following:

1 Topsoil is dark in colour.

______

2 Clayey soil has little air.

______

Very Short Answer Type Questions

1 On what does the nature of any soil depend?

______

2 Which layer of soil has the highest proportion of humus?

______

3 Write the composition of Loamy soil.

______

Short Answer Type Questions

1 What is the importance of soil? Why is it considered an indispensable part of our life?

______

2 What is the role of A-horizon?

______

Long Answer Type Questions

1 Fill in the box given below with suitable sentences under each heading:

Soil type	Composition	Properties
(a) Sandy soil	I ______	(i) ______
(b) Clayey soil	II ______	(ii) ______
(c) Loamy soil	III ______	(iii) ______

2 Label the different horizons in the given figure of soil. Also, write the characteristic of each horizon.

Worksheet 2 Soil: Properties and its Erosion

True/False

1 Write 'T' for True or 'F' for False for the following statements:

(a) The percolation rate of water is highest in clayey soil. ☐

(b) Air above the soil seems to shimmer due to presence of water in soil. ☐

(c) All types of soil absorb water to same extent. ☐

(d) The climatic factors solely determine the type of vegetation in a region. ☐

(e) Wheat crops are grown in fine clayey soils. ☐

(f) Soil erosion can be prevented by increasing the green cover. ☐

Fill in the Blanks

1 Fill in the blanks by using the suitable words:

(a) Soil contains water in it, which is called __________.

(b) On heating, the water in the soil gets __________.

(c) __________ grows in soil having good capacity to retain water.

(d) __________ grows in soil which can hold plenty of air.

(e) Clayey soil are rich in __________ and are very __________.

(f) Plant __________ bind the soil firmly.

Multiple Choice Questions (MCQs)

1 Percolation rate of water in soil is expressed in the unit of

(a) mL/min (b) mg/min (c) mL/g (d) cm/sec

2 Which type of soil can lead to the maximum water-logging in the fields?

(a) Loamy soil (b) Clayey soil

(c) Sandy soil (d) Sandy-loam soil

3 Following are the cities famous for Sohagpuri *surahis* and *matkas*.

I. Delhi II. Nagpur

III. Allahabad IV. Jabalpur

Choose the correct option:

(a) Both I and II (b) Both II and III

(c) Both III and IV (d) II, III and IV

4 Soil conservation measures are mainly aimed at protecting

(a) plants (b) top soil

(c) subsoil (d) soil organisms

Define the following terms:

1 Percolation ____________________

2 Soil moisture ____________________

3 Water retention ____________________

4 Soil erosion ____________________

Give reasons for the following:

1 Horse dung is mixed in soil used for making *surahis* and *matkas*.

____

2 On a hot summer day, the air above the farmland (soil) is shimmering.

____

Very Short Answer Type Questions

1 Write down the formula for calculating the percentage of water absorbed.

____

2 On what factor does the water retention capacity of soil depend?

____

Short Answer Type Questions

1 If the percolation rate of water of a particular soil sample is 20 mL/min, then how much time will 200 mL of water take to percolate completely into the soil?

2 Write down the physical properties of soil that are important for growing crops.

Long Answer Type Questions

1 (a) Which factors affect the soil profile?

(b) Different types of crops are grown in different types of soils. Justify with suitable examples.

2 State the various causes of soil erosion and their effects on vegetation.

SUMMATIVE ASSESSMENT

BASED ON COMPLETE CHAPTER .....

Multiple Choice Questions (MCQs) (1 mark each)

1 The microorganisms present in the soil require moisture (water) and nutrients for growth and survival. Choose from the options below, the habitat (place) where the soil has plenty of water and nutrients.

(a) desert (b) forest (c) open field (d) cricket ground

2 Apparatus like dropper, filter paper, funnel and a beaker are used during

(a) measuring the rate of percolation of soil

(b) working with the soil

(c) removing moisture from the soil

(d) measuring the absorption of water in the soil

3 Read the following statements with reference to clayey soil.

I. Clay soil is used to make pots and toys.
II. Water can drain quickly through clayey soil.
III. Rate of percolation is highest in clayey soil.
IV. Clay soil is composed of fine particles.

Choose the correct statements from the above statements.

(a) I and II (b) II and III (c) III and IV (d) I and IV

4 The proportion of sand, silt and clay in a soil sample determines the

(a) structure (b) texture
(c) nutrient potential (d) fertility level

5 Which of the following does not cause erosion of soil?

(a) Deforestation (b) Fragmentation of rocks
(c) Floods (d) Overgrazing

Very Short Answer Type Questions (1 mark each)

1 State two measures to prevent soil erosion.

2 A 150 g soil sample is dried completely by keeping it under the sun. The weight of the dried soil is 135 g. Calculate the percentage of water (or moisture) in the given sample of soil.

$$\left[\text{Use formula: \% of water in soil} = \frac{\text{Volume of water in soil absorbed}}{\text{Original mass of soil}} \times 100\right]$$

3 What is soil conservation?

4 Name any two crops that are suitable to grow in black soil.

5 How do plants help in the formation of soil?

Short Answer Type I Questions (2 marks each)

1 Enlist the important uses of soil.

2 Can we make a pot with sandy soil? Give reason for your answer.

Short Answer Type II Questions (3 marks each)

1 (a) What type of soil is required for growing lentil (*Masoor dal*) and other pulses?

(b) Which of the two provides more air to plant roots: Sandy soil or clayey soil? Why?

(c) Explain, why soil covered with vegetation does not erode easily but the bare soil does so easily?

2 How is loamy soil very useful for the crops?

Long Answer Type Questions (5 marks each)

1 Anjali took a handful of garden soil and put it in a glass. She then added some water into it and mixed it well. Afterwards she allowed it to settle. In what order, the soil components will get arranged in this glass?
Draw the different layers of soil formed and also label them.

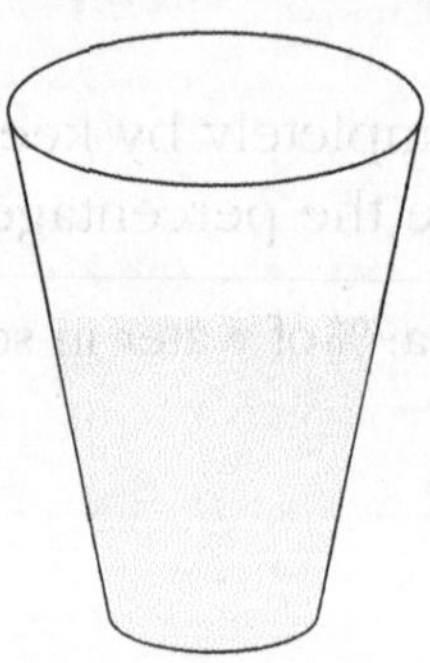

2 Generally, in towns and cities, the bore wells have to be dug very deep to get water as compared to bore wells dug in villages. Give suitable reasons.

ACTIVITY 1 (Word Search)

Several terms related to soil are hidden in the squares given figure. Spot them and make a list. Two examples are given for you.

G	R	P	E	L	I	F	O	R	P
W	H	U	M	U	S	S	G	M	E
E	A	B	S	R	G	A	I	G	R
A	E	T	C	G	V	N	K	N	C
T	R	H	E	G	E	D	Z	C	O
H	O	E	D	R	O	C	K	S	L
E	S	P	A	A	A	K	P	C	A
R	I	L	D	V	R	S	I	L	T
I	O	A	K	E	G	Q	M	A	I
N	N	N	T	L	S	G	H	Y	O
G	K	T	H	O	R	I	Z	O	N

ACTIVITY 2 (Jumbled Words)

Unscramble the following jumbled words related to soil.

(i) S U H U M

(ii) I L O S F I P R O L E

(iii) Z O I N O R H

(iv) M O A L

(v) G I N R H E T W E A

(vi) A T O N I E R P C L

Chapter 10

Respiration in Organisms

Worksheet 1 Respiration Types and Process in Humans

Fill in the Blanks

1 Fill in the blanks with the suitable words:

(a) All living organisms __________ to get energy from food.

(b) In the cells, __________ inhaled from the air helps in the breakdown of food.

(c) __________ are single celled organisms that can survive in the absence of air and so, they are called anaerobes.

(d) During deficiency of oxygen, our __________ cells respire anaerobically.

(e) When we exercise, we __________ faster.

(f) Breathing involves movement of __________ and __________.

True/False

1 Write 'T' for True or 'F' for False for the following statements:

(a) Energy can be released in some cells without oxygen. ☐

(b) Oxygen breaks down glucose outside the cells of organism. ☐

(c) The size of chest cavity increases during inhalation. ☐

(d) Exhaled air has more percentage of CO_2 than inhaled air. ☐

(e) In human body, O_2 and CO_2 are exchanged in the lungs. ☐

(f) Diaphragm forms the floor of the chest cavity. ☐

Multiple Choice Questions (MCQs)

1 Yeast is used in brewing industries because it respires

(a) aerobically producing oxygen

(b) aerobically producing alcohol

(c) anaerobically producing alcohol

(d) anaerobically producing CO_2

2 Which of the following is the equation for aerobic respiration in humans?
(a) Glucose → Alcohol + Energy
(b) Glucose → Lactic acid + Energy
(c) Glucose + Oxygen → Energy + Carbon dioxide + Water
(d) Glucose + Carbon dioxide → Oxygen + Energy + Water

3 When Shubhanker went to the gym and ran on the treadmill, he got cramps. This happened due to
(a) lack of oxygen
(b) excess exhalation caused more CO_2 to be exhaled
(c) accumulation of lactic acid
(d) less glucose production

4 The normal range of breathing rate per minute of an average adult person at rest is
(a) 9-12
(b) 15-18
(c) 21-24
(d) 30-33

5 During the process of exhalation, the ribs move
(a) down and inwards
(b) up and inwards
(c) down and outwards
(d) up and downwards

Matching Type

1 Match the gas in column I with its composition in column II:

Column I (*Gas*)	Column II (*Characteristic*)
(a) Carbon dioxide	(i) 21% of inhaled air
(b) Oxygen	(ii) 0.04% of inhaled air
	(iii) Breaks glucose during respiration
	(iv) 16.4% of exhaled air
	(v) Turns lime water milky
	(vi) 4.4% of exhaled air

Explain the following terms:

1 Anaerobes ____________________

2 Breathing rate ____________________

3 Nasal cavity ____________________

4 Windpipe ____________________

5 Diaphragm ____________________

Differentiate between the following:

1 Aerobic and Anaerobic respiration

2 Inhalation and Exhalation

3 Breathing and Respiration

Very Short Answer Type Questions

1 What do you understand by cellular respiration?

2 Write down the products of anaerobic respiration in yeast.

3 What is present in exhaled air apart from carbon dioxide and oxygen?

4 Name one bad habit which can cause lung cancer.

Short Answer Type Questions

1 What is a cell? What are its functions in our body?

2 Why do we get relief from cramps after a hot water bath?

3 The breathing rate, may differ under different conditions. Arrange the following activities given in the box in order of increasing breathing rates and give reason for your answer.

sleeping	*cycling*	*brisk walk*	*watching TV*

4 Why do we sneeze?

Long Answer Type Questions

1 Observe the given figure carefully and answer the following questions:

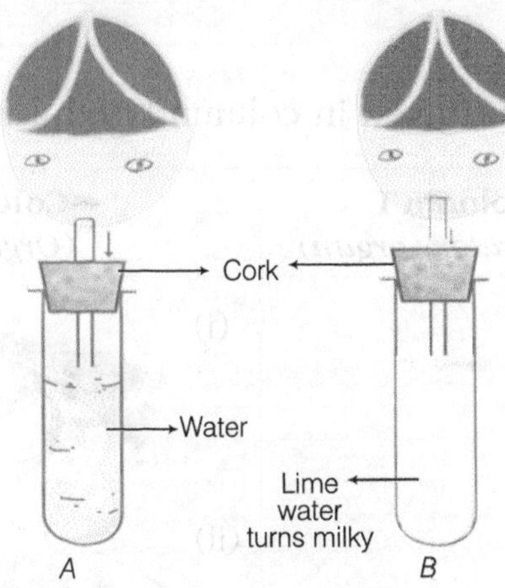

(a) Which process is being tested in the activity?

(b) What is the result of the activity? Give reasons.

2 Observe the figure given below and label its parts *A*, *B*, *C*, *D*, *E*, *F* and *G*. Also, explain the mechanism of breathing in humans.

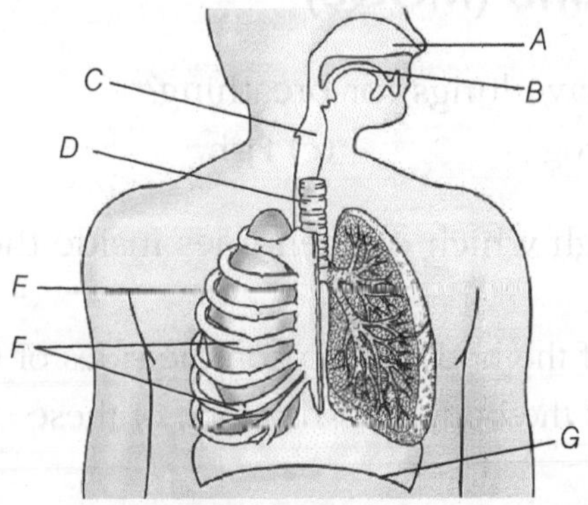

Worksheet 2 Breathing in Other Organisms

Matching Type

1 Match the respiratory organs given in column I with the figure given in column II:

Column I (*Respiratory organ*)	**Column II** (*Organism*)
(a) Stomata	(i) 
(b) Skin	(ii) 
(c) Tracheae	(iii) 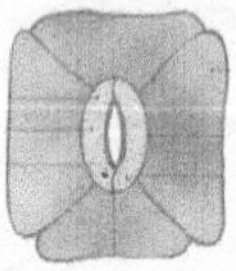
(d) Gills	(iv) 

Multiple Choice Questions (MCQs)

1 Which animal does not have lungs for breathing?

(a) Humans (b) Frog (c) Fish (d) Fox

2 The small opening through which oxygen goes inside the body of a cockroach are present

(a) on the upper portion of the body (b) on the sides of the body

(c) on the lower portion of the body (d) None of these

3 Gills in fishes are

(a) projections of the skin (b) extra-respiratory organ

(c) Both (a) and (b) (d) None of these

4 Roots take up air from the

(a) stomata present on them

(b) exchanging CO_2 with the leaves

(c) air spaces present between the soil particles

(d) All of the above

True/False

1 Write 'T' for True or 'F' for False for the following statements:

(a) Cockroaches breathe with the help of special air tubes in their body. ☐

(b) Frogs can breathe through their skin as well as lungs. ☐

(c) Fishes breathe through a blow hole in their fins. ☐

(d) Goat is an organism with tracheal system. ☐

(e) In plants, carbon dioxide is used to breakdown glucose. ☐

Fill in the Blanks

1 Fill in the blanks by using the words given in the box:

upwards	*blood vessels*	*Earthworms*	*Dolphins*	*blow holes*
slippery	*whales*	*oxygen*	*water*	*moist*

(a) __________ and frogs breathe through their skin because of which the skin of both the organisms is __________ and __________.

(b) Fish breathe with the help of gills which are richly supplied with __________. The gills help the fish to take in __________ dissolved in __________.

(c) __________ and __________ often come up to the water surface. They even release a fountain of water sometimes while moving __________. They have __________ to breathe in air.

Define the following terms:

1 Tracheae ______________________________

2 Gills ______________________________

Name the respiratory organ of the following:

1 Birds

____

2 Earthworms

____

3 Lizards

____

Very Short Answer Type Questions

1 Which respiratory organ do we need to breathe under water?

____

2 Give the products of breakdown of glucose in plant cells.

____

Short Answer Type Questions

1 On a very cold morning, Boojho and Paheli were talking with each other as they walked down to their school. They observed that the air coming out of their mouth looked like smoke. They were amused and wondered, how it happened? What do you think could be the reason?

2 Insects and leaves of a plant have special openings through which gaseous exchange takes place. These openings have different characteristics in both cases. Complete the table below, based on these differences.

Insect	OPENINGS FOR GAS EXCHANGE	Leaf
	Name	
	Position	
	Gases exchange	
	Extension into the body	

Long Answer Type Questions

1 Describe the process of breathing in cockroach and earthworm.

2 (a) Draw a diagram showing absorption of air from the soil by roots.

(b) Label the parts in (a).

(c) Explain respiration in roots with the help of diagram (a).

SUMMATIVE ASSESSMENT

BASED ON COMPLETE CHAPTER.....

Multiple Choice Questions (MCQs) (1 mark each)

1 Breathing is a process that

I. provides O_2 to the body.

II. breaks down food to release energy.

III. helps the body to get rid of CO_2.

IV. produces water in the cells.

Which of the following gives the correct combination of functions of breathing?

(a) Both I and II
(b) Both II and III
(c) Both I and III
(d) Both II and IV

2 When we breathe in air, we also take in dust, smoke, pollens, etc. How does the body deal with these unwanted particles?

(a) The lungs absorbs these and send them out as waste
(b) These things are exhaled out instantly
(c) They get trapped in the tiny hairs in the nose
(d) The volume of the lungs increases by them

3 The diagram below shows a model of the human respiratory system.

What do the glass tube, bell jar, balloons and rubber sheet represent?

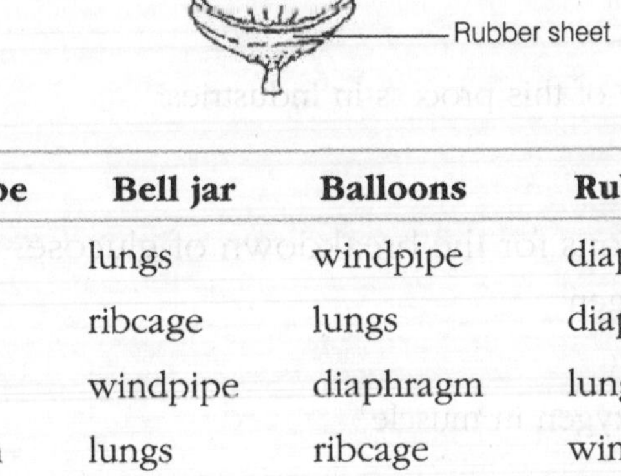

	Glass tube	Bell jar	Balloons	Rubber sheet
(a)	ribcage	lungs	windpipe	diaphragm
(b)	windpipe	ribcage	lungs	diaphragm
(c)	ribcage	windpipe	diaphragm	lungs
(d)	diaphragm	lungs	ribcage	windpipe

4 The percentage of oxygen to carbon dioxide in inhaled air is

(a) 21 : 0.04 (b) 15 : 12.5 (c) 16.4 : 4.4 (d) 15.8 : 6.9

5 Name the organ of the body in which the blood is oxygenated.

(a) heart (b) lungs (c) liver (d) pancreas

Very Short Answer Type Questions (1 mark each)

1 Why is it advised to cover our nose while sneezing?

2 State the role of blood in the process of respiration.

3 What is the source of energy for cell to perform activity like nutrition, transport, excretion, etc?

4 Why do we feel hungry after a physical activity like a game of cricket?

5 Whenever we feel drowsy or sleepy, we start yawning. Does yawning help us in anyway?

Short Answer Type I Questions (2 marks each)

1 Arjun carried out an experiment as shown in the set up below:

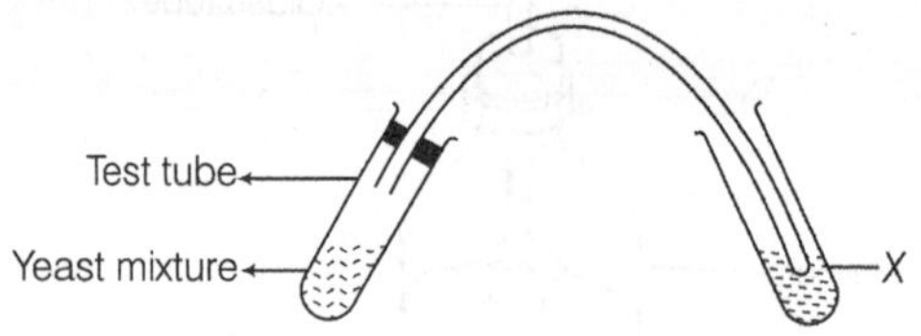

(a) Name the liquid in test tube *X*.

(b) What is the purpose of this process in industries?

2 Write down the equations for the breakdown of glucose:

(a) With the use of oxygen

(b) In the absence of oxygen in muscle

Short Answer Type II Questions (3 marks each)

1 Write the differences between photosynthesis and respiration in plants.

2 Explain the path the air we breathe in takes.

Long Answer Type Questions (5 marks each)

1 "Respiration is a vital biological process". Justify the statement.

2 Observe the figures *A* and *B* given below and answer the following questions:

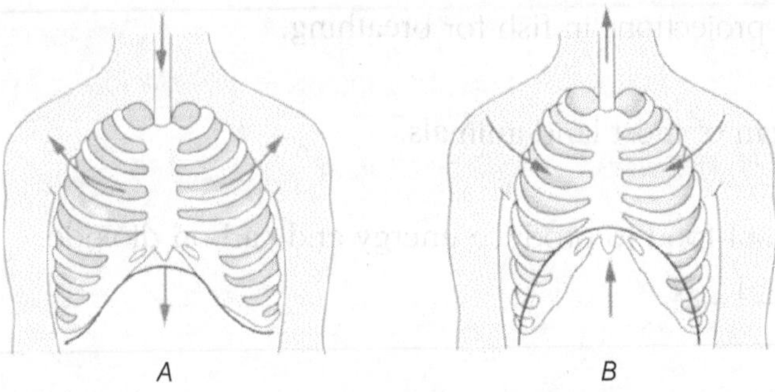

(a) Name the process taking place in *A* and *B*.

(b) Explain the mechanism of *A* and *B*.

(c) What do the arrows indicate in the figures?

ACTIVITY 1 (Word Identification)

Complete the following words:

(i) The going out of air rich in carbon dioxide

_ _ _ _ _ _ _ _ _ O _

(ii) The muscular sheet which forms the floor of chest cavity.

_ _ _ _ _ _ R _ _ M

(iii) The air tubes found only in insects.

_ _ _ CH_ _ _

(iv) The openings of our nose.

_ _ _ _ R _ _ _

(v) The gas produced in plants as a result of respiration.

_ _ _ _ _ N_ _ _ X _ _ _

(vi) Fine hair like projections in fish for breathing.

_ I _ _ _

(vii) Breathing organ of most land animals.

_ _ _ G _

(viii) The oxidation of food to produce energy and carbon dioxide.

_ _ _ _ _ _ _ _ _ I _ N

ACTIVITY 2 (Experiment)

Observe the given set up and answer the questions given below.

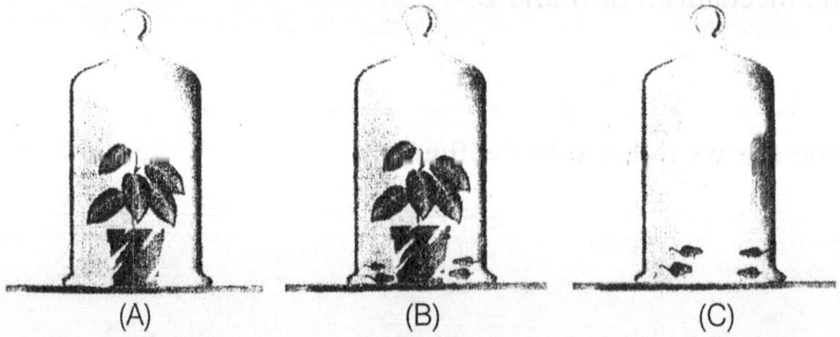

(a) In which jar, will the amount of CO_2 be the highest and why?

(b) In which jar, will the amount of CO_2 be the lowest and why?

Chapter 11

Transportation in Animals and Plants

Worksheet 1 Circulatory System

Multiple Choice Questions (MCQs)

1 What is the basic need of all the living organisms?

(a) They need food, water and oxygen for survival

(b) A circulatory system with heart in the body

(c) An excretory system for transport of substances

(d) None of the above

2 The blood of a person is lacking haemoglobin. Which of the following statement would be incorrect in this case?

(a) The colour of the blood will be red

(b) Blood will carry oxygen to the cell efficiently

(c) Both (a) and (b)

(d) None of the above

3 During an injury, which blood cell will prevent excess loss of blood from the body?

(a) Red blood cells (b) White blood cells

(c) Platelets (d) Plasma

4 If a person wants to feel his pulse, he should place his fingers on

(a) temple (b) wrist

(c) neck (d) All of these

5 The absorption of nutrients and exchange of respiratory gases between blood and tissues takes place in

(a) veins (b) arteries

(c) heart (d) capillaries

6 Among the blood vessels given below, which of the following carry carbon dioxide rich blood?

I. Pulmonary artery
II. Vena cava
III. Pulmonary vein

Choose the correct option:

(a) Both I and II (b) Both II and III (c) Both I and III (d) Only III

7 The prevention of backflow of blood inside the heart during contraction is done by

(a) thick muscular walls of ventricles
(b) valves
(c) thin walls of atria
(d) All of these

Matching Type

1 Match the parts of the heart in column I with the direction of flow of blood in column II:

Column I (*Parts of the heart*)	Column II (*Direction of flow of blood*)
(a) Right ventricle	(i) Pushes blood into the pulmonary artery
(b) Left atrium	(ii) Receives blood from different parts of the body
(c) Left ventricle	(iii) Pushes blood into the aorta
(d) Right auricle	(iv) Receives deoxygenated blood from the pulmonary vein

True/False

1 Write 'T' for True or 'F' for False for the following statements:

(a) Arteries have thin walls while veins have thick walls. ☐
(b) The heart is located in the chest cavity with its lower tip slightly titled towards the left. ☐
(c) Human heart has two chambers, an atrium and a ventricle. ☐
(d) The upper chamber of the heart is called vena cava. ☐
(e) The largest artery is aorta while largest vein is vena cava. ☐
(f) Pulmonary veins brings oxygenated blood from lungs to the heart. ☐

Fill in the Blanks

1 Fill in the blanks of the following paragraph using just two words, i.e. **arteries** and veins:

____(a)____ carry oxygen-rich blood from the heart to all parts of the body and ____(b)____ carry carbon dioxide-rich blood from all parts of the body back to the heart. ____(c)____ have thin walls and ____(d)____ have thick elastic walls. Blood flows at high pressure in ____(e)____. Valves are present in ____(f)____ which allow blood to flow only towards the heart. ____(g)____ divide into smaller vessels. These vessels further divide into extremely thin tubes called capillaries. The capillaries join up to form ____(h)____.

Give reasons for the following:

1 Blood is red in colour.

2 We feel throbbing movements when we place our fingers on the wrist.

3 There is partition separating the two halves of our heart.

Answer the following statements in one word:

1 The fluid part of the blood.

2 The red pigment which carries oxygen in the blood.

3 The blood cells which fight against germs.

4 The blood vessels which connect the arteries to veins.

5 Carry blood away from the heart.

6 Carry blood towards the heart.

Define the following terms:

1 Platelets

2 Capillaries

3 Heart

4 Atria

5 Ventricles

Differentiate between the following:

1 Red blood cells and White blood cells

2 Arteries and Veins

Very Short Answer Type Questions

1 What is the size of a human heart?

2 Give examples of animals without a circulatory system.

3 Name the physician who discovered circulation of blood.

Short Answer Type Questions

1 (a) What do you understand by pulse and pulse rate?

(b) What is the pulse rate of a normal person at rest?

2 Write a note on "Discovery of circulation of blood".

3 How does circulation in sponges and *Hydra* take place?

Long Answer Type Questions

1 What is blood? How does it carry various substances?

2 (a) Given below is a figure showing section of a human heart. Label its parts *A* to *I*.

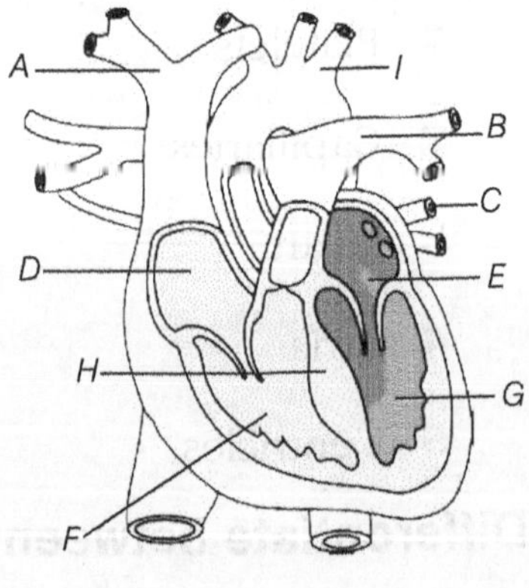

(b) Mention the sides of the heart that carry oxygenated blood and deoxygenated blood respectively.

3 Define heart beat. If a doctor wants to check your heart beat, which instrument would he use and how? Also, draw the instrument.

Worksheet 2 Excretion in Animals

Fill in the Blanks

1 Fill in the blanks using the words, i.e. **blood and kidney** in the paragraph below:

The waste which is present in the ______(a)______ has to be removed from the body. Thus, our body needs a mechanism to filter the ______(b)______. This is done by the ______(c)______ capillaries in the ______(d)______. When the ______(e)______ reaches the two ______(f)______, it contains both useful and harmful substances. The useful substances are absorbed back into the ______(g)______. The wastes are removed as urine.

True/False

1 Write 'T' for True or 'F' for False for the following statements:

(a) Filtration of blood takes place in the kidney. ☐

(b) Ureter connects the kidney to the urinary bladder. ☐

(c) The structure of urethra is like a cup. ☐

(d) We produce more urine during summer. ☐

(e) Sweat is a waste product of our body. ☐

(f) Sweat contains salt and water. ☐

(g) Lizards excrete waste as semi-solid white coloured compound. ☐

Multiple Choice Questions (MCQs)

1 The correct number of parts of the human excretory system are

(a) 2 urethra, 2 kidneys, 1 urinary bladder and ureter

(b) 2 kidneys, 2 ureters, a urinary bladder and 1 urethra

(c) 2 ureters, 2 urethra and 1 urinary bladder

(d) 2 urethra, 2 urinary bladder and 1 kidney

2 The urine we excrete is stored in

(a) kidney (b) bladder

(c) ureter (d) urethra

3 The procedure of cleaning of blood of a person by using a kidney machine is known as

(a) ketolysis (b) hydrolysis

(c) dialysis (d) photolysis

4 In which of the following parts of human body, sweat glands are absent?

(a) Head (b) Armpits

(c) Lips (d) Palms

Matching Type

1 Match the following excretory substance in column I with the animal that excretes it in column II:

Column I (*Excretory substance*)	**Column II** (*Animals*)
(a) Ammonia	(i) Birds
(b) Urea	(ii) Snakes
(c) Uric acid	(iii) Human
(d) Sweat	(iv) Fishes

Define the following terms:

1 Excretion ______

2 Excretory system ______

3 Kidneys ______

4 Urinary bladder ______

5 Ureters ______

Very Short Answer Type Questions

1 How much urine does a normal person pass out in 24 hours?

______

2 Why do we get white patches on our clothes on a hot summer day?

______

3 Choose the odd one out and justify the correct choice:

(a) Sweat, urine, oxygen, carbon dioxide

______

(b) Urine, ureter, urethra, urinary bladder

______

(c) Birds, lizards, snake, fishes

______

Short Answer Type Questions

1 Write down the constituents of urine.

______

2 Why do we sweat?

____

3 What will happen, if a person's kidney stops working? Name the process which can correct this problem.

____

Long Answer Type Question

1 Why is it necessary to excrete waste products?

____

____

Worksheet 3 Transportation in Plants

Fill in the Blanks

1 Fill in the blanks by using words given in the box below, but first unscramble the words. (Note: Single word can be used twice)

slarenim	*facesur reaa*	*hria toor*	*terwa*	*oils*

Plants absorb water and ______(a)______ by the roots. The roots have ______(b)______. These increase the ______(c)______ of the root for the absorption of ______(d)______ and ______(e)______ nutrients dissolved in ______(f)______. The ______(g)______ is in contact with the ______(h)______ present between the ______(i)______ particles.

2 Fill in the blanks with the suitable words:

(a) Leaves prepare food for the plant with the help of ________ and ________ during photosynthesis.

(b) Cell of an organism gets energy by the breakdown of ________.

(c) Plants have pipe-like ________ for transport of substances.

(d) Transpiration is nothing, but ________ of water from leaves.

(e) ________ cools the plants.

Multiple Choice Questions (MCQs)

1 The plants part which takes part in uptake of mineral nutrient dissolved in water is

(a) xylem (b) phloem

(c) root (d) root hair

2 Look at the figure given below carefully:
Which of the following correctly matches the substances carried in the direction of arrows *P* and *Q* ?

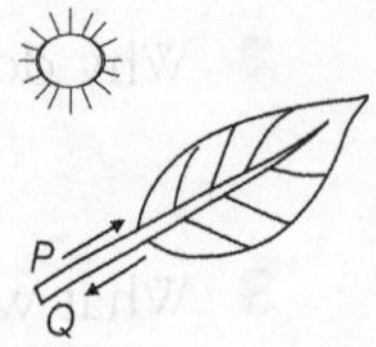

	P	*Q*
(a)	Water	Sugar
(b)	Carbon dioxide	Oxygen
(c)	Water vapour	Carbon dioxide
(d)	Sugar	Water

3 Refer to the figure and identify which polythene bag contains water droplets and why?

(a) Polythene *X* because transpiration takes place through leaves
(b) Polythene *Y* because transpiration takes place through stems
(c) Polythene *X* because photosynthesis takes place through leaves
(d) Polythene *Y* because respiration takes place through stems

4 In a tall tree, the force responsible for pulling water and minerals upward is
(a) gravitational force
(b) transportation force
(c) suction force
(d) conduction force

True/False

1 Given below are substances present in plant. Write True under the heading by which these substance gets transported in plant, and False under which it does not:

Substance	Xylem	Phloem
(a) Glucose		
(b) Water		
(c) Mineral nutrients		
(d) Other sugars		
(e) Oils		

Define the following terms:

1 Tissue ______________________

2 Root hair ______________________

3 Transpiration ______________________

Very Short Answer Type Questions

1 Why food prepared by leaves is carried to other parts of the plant?

____

2 Name the channel that connects roots to the leaves through the stem.

3 Name the part of leaf without which transpiration cannot take place.

Short Answer Type Questions

1 How does the movement of food in plants differ from the movement of water in it?

2 Differentiate between xylem and phloem.

3 Does transpiration serve any useful function in a plant? Explain.

Long Answer Type Questions

1 Explain the movement of water from the soil particles to xylem vessels in the centre of a root.

2 "Plants also have a transport system". Is it true? If yes, name the parts of plants that form this system and the need of it for the plant.

SUMMATIVE ASSESSMENT

BASED ON COMPLETE CHAPTER .....

Multiple Choice Questions (MCQs) (1 mark each)

1 Blood travels from your toe to finger. Which is the correct option showing the path taken by the blood during this travel?

(a) Toe --> heart --> lungs --> heart --> finger

(b) Toe --> heart --> lungs --> finger --> heart

(c) Toe --> lungs --> heart --> finger --> heart

(d) Toe --> lungs --> heart --> lungs --> finger

2 The given bar chart shows the concentration of oxygen in blood samples at four places in the circulatory system of a man. Which sample was taken from the pulmonary artery?

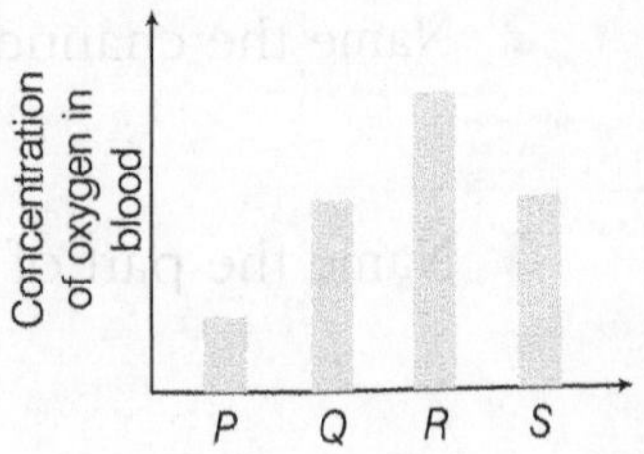

(a) *P* (b) *Q* (c) *R* (d) *S*

3 Given below is the diagram of human excretory system.
Which of the following parts, *X*, *Y* or *Z*, if gets damaged leads to dialysis?

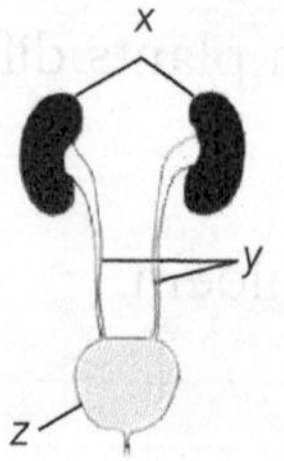

(a) *X* (b) *Y* (c) *Z* (d) None of these

4 Read the features of plant parts given below: They are pipe-like, consisting of a group of specialised cells.
They transport substances and form a two-way traffic in plants. Which of the following terms qualify for the features mentioned above?

(a) Xylem tissue (b) Vascular tissue
(c) Root hair (d) Phloem tissue

5 Karan set up an experiment in a room for which he takes 500 mL of water each in two beakers *X* and *Y*. Then a plant was placed in *X* as shown in the given diagram. The height of the water level in both *X* and *Y* was recorded every day for a week. The results were presented in a graph. Which graph correctly shows the changes in water level in both *X* and *Y*?

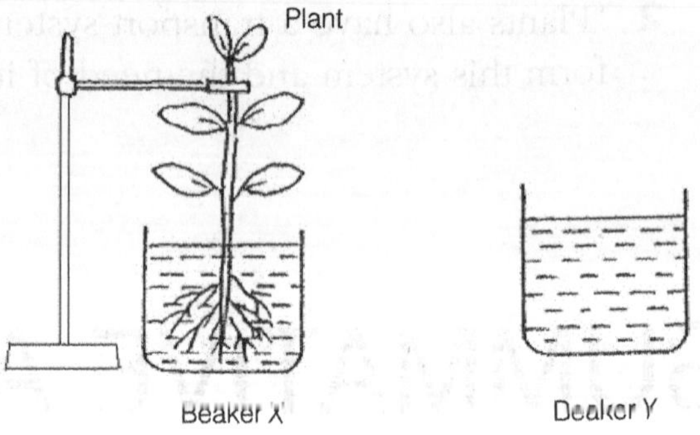

(a)
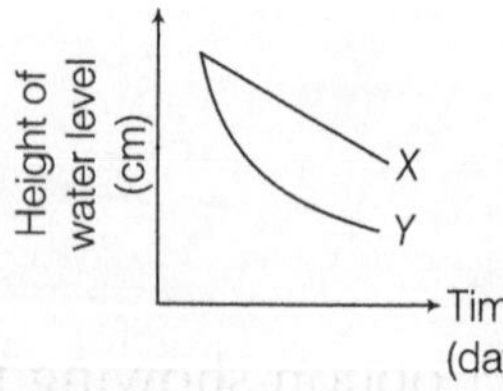

(b)
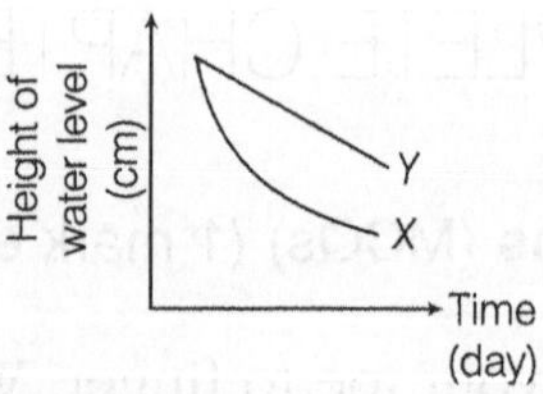

(c)
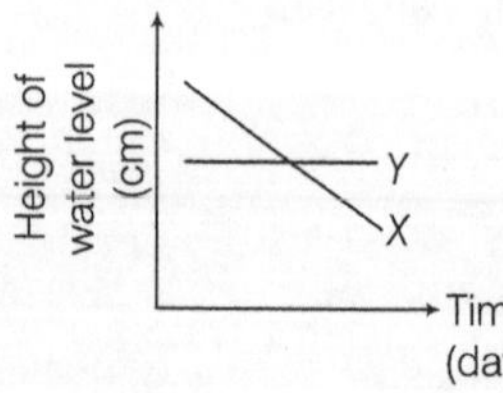

(d)
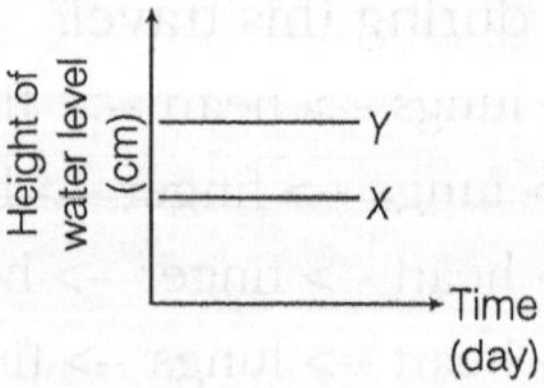

Very Short Answer Type Questions (1 mark each)

1 If the pulse rate of an athlete is 95 per minute, what is the number of his heart beats in the same time?

2 Veins have valves which allow blood to flow only in one direction. Arteries do not have valves, but the blood flows in one direction only. Explain, why?

3 What will happen if oxygenated and deoxygenated blood get mixed?

4 If a person drinks very little water during the day, the quantity of urine passed by him decreases. Which important body waste will not be flushed out properly under these conditions?

5 Name the process and the organ which helps in removing the following wastes from the body.

(a) Carbon dioxide

(b) Undigested food

Short Answer Type I Questions (2 marks each)

1 What is the purpose of rhythmic beating of heart?

2 What is the average number of heart beats per minute of an adult person while resting? Explain, why the heart beats faster during and after an exercise?

Short Answer Type II Questions (3 marks each)

1 There is no substitute for blood. Do you agree? Give reasons for your answer.

2 Study the given flowchart and answer the following.

What do the symbols *P*, *Q* and *R* represent? Also, write down their role in plant.

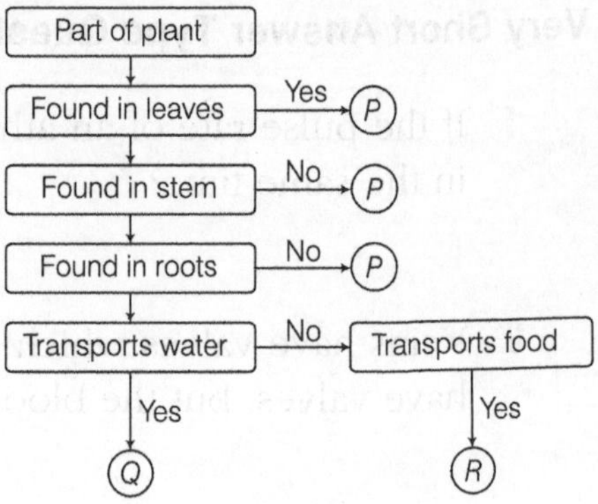

Long Answer Type Questions (5 marks each)

1 Given below is a simplified diagram of the circulatory system of man. The arrows represent the circulation of blood in the body.

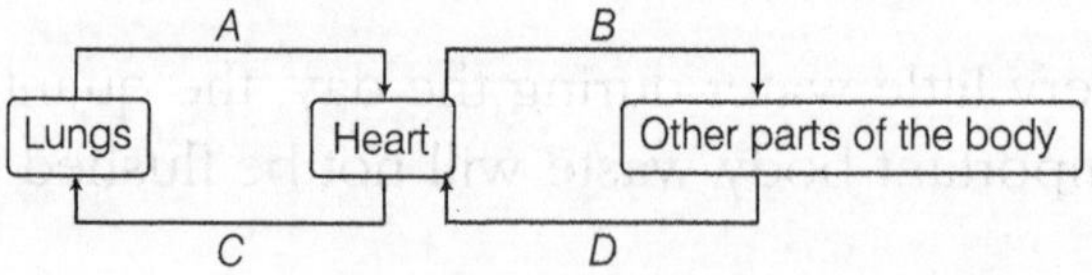

(a) Name the vessels *A*, *B*, *C* and *D*. Which blood vessel contains the greatest amount of carbon dioxide?

(b) Explain the functioning of circulatory system.

2 Read the following terms given below:

Arteries	*Xylem*	*Kidneys*	*Veins*
Atria	*Root hair*	*Capillaries*	*Phloem*
Heart	*Ureter*	*Urinary bladder*	*Urethra*

Group the terms on the basis of the categories given below and also write their functions:

(a) Circulatory system of animals.

(b) Excretory system in humans.

(c) Transport of substances in plants.

ACTIVITY (Jumbled Word)

1 Unscramble the following word using the hints given below:

(i) A vascular tissue in plant which translocates/transports glucose.
MELHOP

(ii) The device used to hear the heartbeats clearly.
OCEHSETTPES

(iii) The blood cells which are responsible for clothing of blood.
TLPASELET

(iv) The blood vessels in which the blood flows at a high pressure.
TRRIEAES

(v) The process by which plants get rid of their wastes.
ROATININSPATR

[Chapter 12]

Reproduction in Plants

Worksheet 1 Asexual Reproduction in Plants

Multiple Choice Questions (MCQs)

1 A characteristic common to all living organisms is

(a) production of new individuals
(b) movement from one place to another
(c) presence of roots, stems and leaves
(d) production of seeds

2 Choose the incorrect statement for reproduction in plants.

(a) It takes place by vegetative parts.
(b) It takes place by reproductive parts.
(c) Sometimes new plants are obtained without seeds or spores.
(d) Only sexual reproduction takes place.

3 What is true for asexual reproduction?

(a) It does not involve gametes
(b) It takes place by fusion of gametes
(c) It may or may not involve gametes
(d) It is a common method of reproduction in animals

4 In asexual reproduction, an organism divides into

(a) two daughter organisms of unequal size
(b) one daughter organism of irregular shape
(c) one or more than one daughter organisms similar to parent
(d) one daughter organism of any size

5 The eye of the potato is important due to the fact that

(a) it can see with its help
(b) seeds grow on it
(c) flowers grow on it
(d) new plants can grow out of it

6 By which method of reproduction, do the algae spread rapidly on a pond with clear water?

(a) Budding
(b) Sexual reproduction
(c) Fragmentation
(d) Pollination

7 Which of these would develop from spores?

I. Ferns II. Apple III. Moss IV. Algae

Choose the correct option:

(a) Both I and II (b) Both II and III (c) Both I and III (d) Both I and IV

Matching Type

1 Match the figures in column I with the correct methods of asexual reproduction in plants in column II:

Column I	Column II
(a) 	(i) Fragmentation
(b) 	(ii) Spore formation
(c) 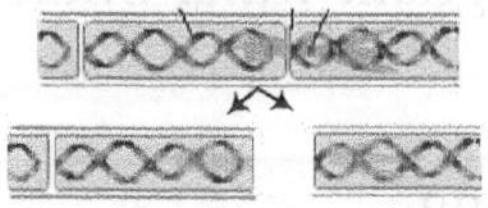	(iii) Vegetative propagation

True/False

1 Write 'T' for True or 'F' for False for the following statements:

(a) Reproduction is the means of continuity of species.

(b) Flowers are sometimes considered the vegetative part of the plant.

(c) Production of new plant without the involvement of fruits is called asexual reproduction.

(d) Asexual reproduction produces exactly the same offspring as the parent.

(e) Buds in potato are also called node.

(f) The small bulb-like projection coming out from the yeast cell is called a bud.

Fill in the Blanks

1 Fill in the blanks by using **stem, roots** or **leaves** in the sentences:

(a) A node is a part of the ________ at which a leaf arises.

(b) *Bryophyllum* can reproduce from its ________.

(c) The ________ of plants like sweet potato can be used to produce new plants.

(d) The ________ of plants normally do not bear buds.

Define the following terms:

1 Cutting ______

2 Fragmentation ______

3 Sporangium ______

Answer the following statements in one word:

1 A plant which can reproduce through stem cutting

______

2 A plant which reproduces through underground stem

______

3 A plant which reproduces by spores

______

Give reasons for the following:

1 We see slimy green patches in ponds or in stagnant water bodies.

______

2 A spore is covered by a hard protective covering.

______

Very Short Answer Type Questions

1 Choose the odd one out and justify the correct choice:

(a) Stem, leaves, flowers, roots ______

(b) Sugarcane, potato, rice, rose ______

2 What are sori in ferns?

______

Short Answer Type Questions

1 Write any two advantages of vegetative propagation in plants.

______

2 Where do the moulds on bread come from?

______

3 Write a short note on fragmentation with a diagram showing the process.

______

Long Answer Type Questions

1 Describe the process of vegetative propagation through different parts of the plant.

2 Explain the process of budding in detail by taking an example of an organism in which it takes place.

Worksheet 2 Sexual Reproduction in Plants

Multiple Choice Questions (MCQs)

1 Which of the following parts of a plant take part in sexual reproduction?

I. Flower II. Seed III. Fruits IV. Branch

Choose the correct answer:

(a) Both I and II (b) I, II and III (c) Both III and IV (d) II, III and IV

2 The ovaries of different flowers may contain

(a) only one ovule (b) many ovules

(c) one to many ovules (d) only two ovules

3 Which of the following is true for flowers?

(a) Flowers are always bisexual

(b) They contain sexual reproductive organs

(c) They are produced in all groups of plants

(d) After fertilisation, they give rise to leaves

4 The figure given below shows the parts of pistil of a flower. Which of the parts labelled *P*, *Q* or *R* eventually develops into a fruit?

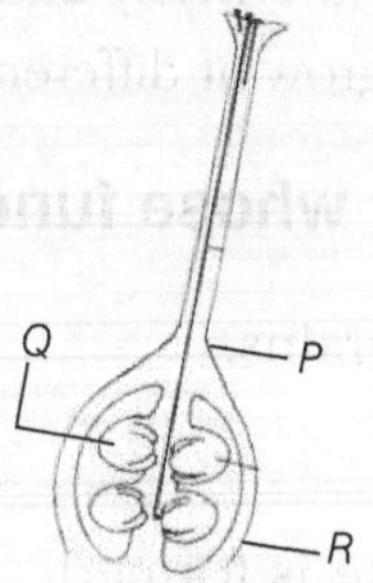

(a) *P* (b) *Q* (c) *R* (d) None of these

5 Which of the following is the correct sequence of events taking place during sexual reproduction in plants?

(a) Pollination, seed, fertilisation, germination

(b) Pollination, fertilisation, seed, germination

(c) Pollination, seed, germination, fertilisation

(d) Pollination, fertilisation, germination, seed

Fill in the Blanks

1 Fill in the blanks with the appropriate words:

The male and female gametes fuse to form a _____(a)_____ during the process of _____(b)_____. This grows into an _____(c)_____ which is enclosed within a seed. After fertilisation, the ovules develop into _____(d)_____ and the ovary develops into a _____(e)_____. Ovules contain _____(f)_____ gamete whereas pollen grains contain _____(g)_____ gamete of the plant.

Matching Type

1 Match the seed types in column I with the characteristic of seed that helps in its dispersal in column II:

Column I	Column II
(a) Drumstick	I. Hairy seeds
(b) *Madar*	II. Wings on seed
(c) Coconut	III. Hooks on seed
(d) *Xanthium*	IV. Spongy outer coat

True/False

1 Write 'T' for True or 'F' for False for the following statements:

(a) Every flower contains both pistil and stamen. ☐

(b) Pollen grains have a tough protective coat which protects them from drying up. ☐

(c) The fruit is a ripened ovary. ☐

(d) Seed is the only structure which develops into a new plant. ☐

(e) Fruits like walnuts and almonds are fleshy and juicy. ☐

(f) In nature, same kind of plants grow at different places. ☐

Give names of the parts of flower whose functions are given below:

1 The part which contains pollen grains.

____

2 The part where the female gamete is formed.

____

3 The female reproductive part where pollen grains germinate.

4 The colourful part of flower which attracts insects.

Define the following terms:

1 Gametes

2 Zygote

3 Ovule

4 Pollen tube

5 Fertilisation

Very Short Answer Type Questions

1 Given below is a list of plants:

papaya	*mustard*	*rose*	*corn*	*Petunia*	*cucumber*

(a) Which of these plants have unisexual flowers?

(b) Which of these plants have bisexual flowers?

2 What are the various parts of

(a) Stamen

(b) Pistil

3 Name the seeds given in figure (i) to (iii) and group them according to their means of dispersal.

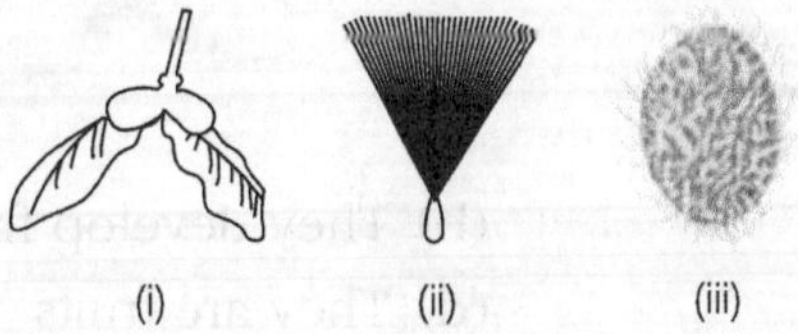

(a) Seed dispersed by wind

(b) Seed dispersed by water

(c) Seed dispersed by animal

Short Answer Type Questions

1 How does the dispersal of seeds in castor and balsam take place?

2 What will happen if all seeds of a plant were to fall at the same place and grow there?

Long Answer Type Questions

1 What is the function of a flower? Why are flowers generally so colourful and fragrant?

2 Describe the phenomenon of pollination. What are its different types? Explain.

SUMMATIVE ASSESSMENT

BASED ON COMPLETE CHAPTER .....

Multiple Choice Questions (MCQs) (1 mark each)

1 In which way, the two figures shown below are similar?

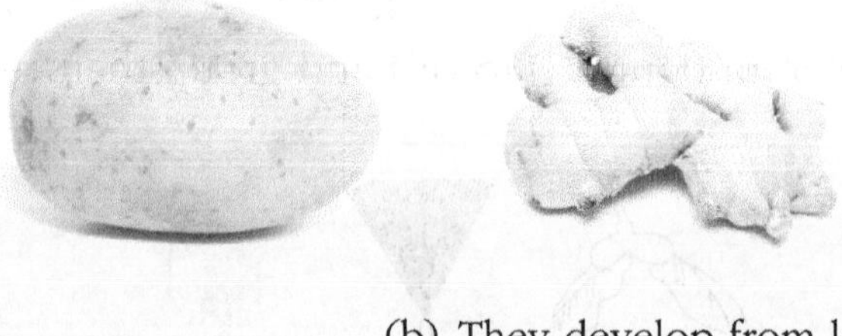

(a) They store food
(b) They develop from leaves
(c) They develop from buds
(d) They are fruits

2 The 'eye' of the potato plant is what
(a) the root is to any plant
(b) the bud is to a flower
(c) the bud is to *Bryophyllum* leaf
(d) the anther is to stamen

3 Which of the following statements is/are true for sexual reproduction in plants?

I. Plants are obtained from seeds
II. Two plants are always essential
III. Fertilisation can occur only after pollination
IV. Only insects are agents of pollination

Choose from the options given below:

(a) Both I and III (b) Only I (c) Both II and III (d) Both I and IV

4 Bees that collect nectar from the flower help carry *X* to other places. Which part of the flower should the bees touch to collect *X*?

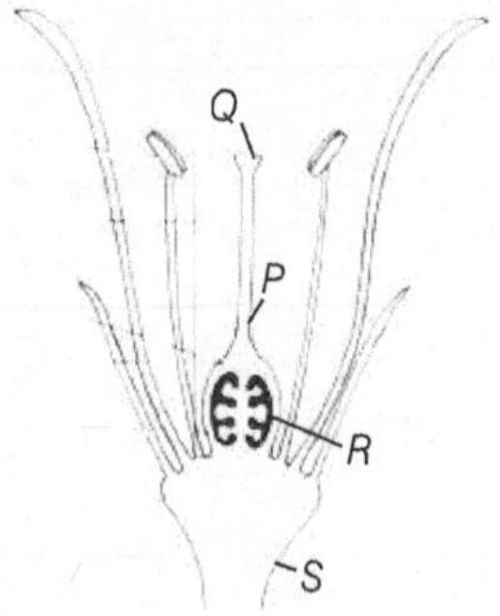

(a) *P* (b) *Q* (c) *R* (d) *S*

5 Look at the given classification chart carefully. How are the following plants grouped?

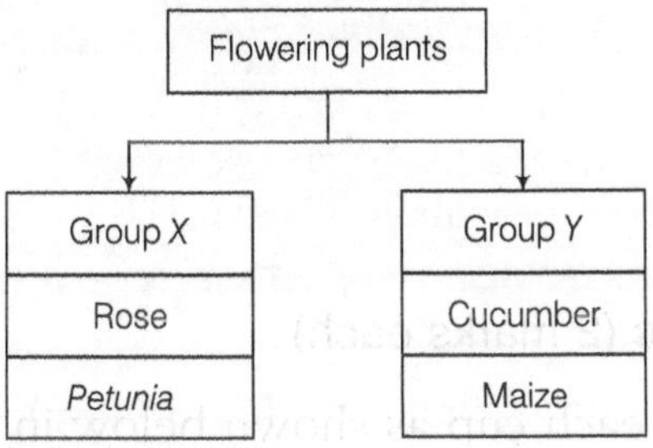

	Group *X*	Group *Y*
(a)	Flowers with both male and female parts	The male and female parts are on separate flowers
(b)	Plants with flowers	Plants without flowers
(c)	Plants without seeds	Plants with seeds
(d)	Reproduction from underground stems	Reproduction from seeds

Very Short Answer Type Questions (1 mark each)

1 Name the type of reproduction.

(a) Involving fusion of gametes

(b) Involving only a single parent

2 Name the type of reproduction in plants carried out

(a) by flowers

(b) without seeds

3 Name a fungus which reproduces

(a) by budding

(b) by spores

4 Name the part of flower.

(a) Male part

(b) Female part

5 Name the structure present in

(a) Pollen grains

(b) Ovules

Short Answer Type I Questions (2 marks each)

1 Ajay placed two seeds in each cup as shown below in the diagram:

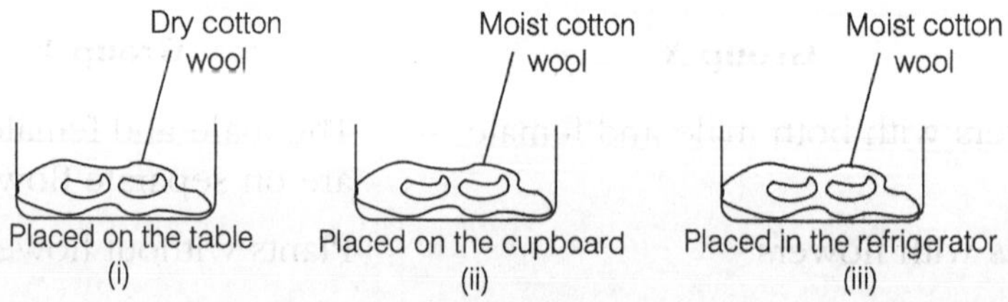

(a) In which cup, the seeds will germinate?

(b) Support your answer in (i) with a reason.

2 How fungus reproduces through spore formation? Explain.

Short Answer Type II Questions (3 marks each)

1 Draw the figures showing:

(a) Pollen grain germination

(b) Zygote formation in plants.

(c) Cross-pollination in plants.

(a)	(b)	(c)

2 What are the functions of fruit?

Long Answer Type Questions (5 marks each)

1 In the diagram of a bisexual flower given in the figure, draw the missing part and name the parts labelled (*a*), (*b*) and (*c*). Write the function of each.

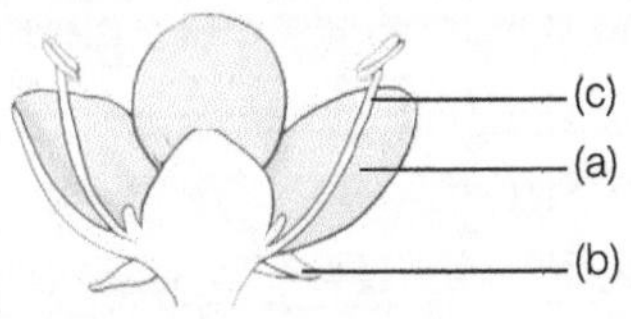

2 What is meant by dispersal of seeds? How do plants benefit from seed dispersal? Explain its different ways with example.

ACTIVITY 1 (Word Identification)

Complete the following words:

(i) Asexual reproductive bodies formed by fungi

_ _ _ _ E

(ii) A flower which is unisexual

_ _ _ _ _ _ _ E _

(iii) A plant which produces spiny seeds with hooks

_ _ E _ _

(iv) A spice which reproduces by bud formation

_ _ _ M _ _ I _

(v) A hard fruit

_ _ _ N _ _

ACTIVITY 2 (Identification)

Given below is a list of ten fruits and vegetables. Write down the fruit bearing part and the mode of dispersal followed by their seeds.

S.No	Name of the plant	Fruit bearing part	Mode of dispersal of seeds
1.	Tomato		
2.	Brinjal		
3.	Coconut		
4.	Chilly		
5.	Mango		
6.	Apple		
7.	Pineapple		
8.	Watermelon		
9.	Bottlegourd		
10.	Cucumber		

[Chapter 13]

Motion and Time

Worksheet 1 Motion and Measurement

Fill in the Blanks

1 Fill in the blanks with the suitable words:

(a) We can differentiate between the motion of two bodies by knowing their __________.

(b) A higher speed seems to indicate that a given __________ has been covered in a short __________.

(c) Average speed of an object is the ratio of total __________ covered to the total __________ taken by an object.

(d) The motion of simple pendulum is __________.

(e) The time measured by __________ clocks is much more accurate than other clocks.

(f) The time taken by the pendulum to complete one oscillation is called its __________.

True/False

1 Write 'T' for True or 'F' for False for the following statements:

(a) The terms 'motion' or 'rest' are relative. ☐

(b) The rate of change of motion is its displacement. ☐

(c) Time is the product of speed and distance. ☐

(d) 10 decades is 10 times more than a century. ☐

(e) The time between one sunrise and the next is called a day. ☐

(f) The symbols of all units must be written in singular. ☐

(g) Speed of body can be expressed in km/h. ☐

(h) Distance covered or moved by a vehicle is measured by odometer. ☐

(i) Speed of a moving car is measured by a device called rpm meter. ☐

Multiple Choice Questions (MCQs)

1 Motion of a car on a straight line with constant speed is

(a) non-uniform motion (b) uniform motion

(c) Both (a) and (b) (d) None of the above

2 A body is in the uniform motion. On which type of path should it travel so that its motion can be called periodic motion.

(a) To and fro (b) Curved path

(c) Straight path (d) None of these

3 Two clocks *A* and *B* are shown in the figures. Clock *A* has an hour and a minute hand, whereas clock *B* has an hour hand, minute hand as well as a second hand. Which of the following statement is correct for these clocks?

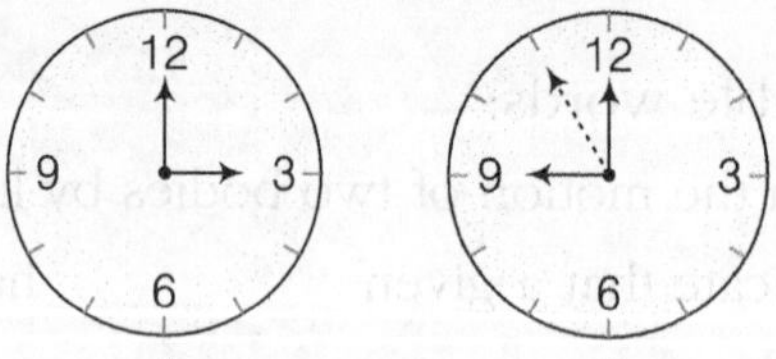

A *B*

(a) A time interval of 30 seconds can be measured by clock *A*

(b) A time interval of 30 seconds cannot be measured by clock *B*

(c) Time interval of 5 minutes can be measured by both *A* and *B*

(d) Time interval of 4 minute 10 second can be measured by clock *A*

4 On which of the following, time period of a simple pendulum depends

(a) length of string (b) mass of bob

(c) Both (a) and (b) (d) None of these

5 Which of the following options is not a standard unit?

(a) Hand span (b) Metre

(c) Second (d) Gram

6 The unit km/h is used to measure

(a) uniform velocity (b) uniform acceleration

(c) speed per unit time (d) distance

7 If we denote speed by S, distance by D and time by T, then the relationship between these quantities is

(a) $S = \frac{D}{T}$ (b) $S \times D = T$

(c) $D \times T = S$ (d) None of these

8 Observe the figure given below. The time period of a simple pendulum is the time taken by it to travel from

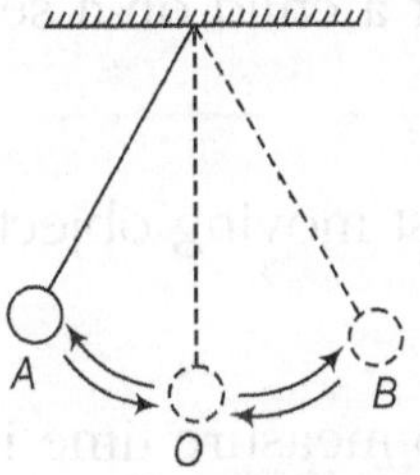

(a) *A* to *B* and back to *A*
(b) *O* to *A*, *A* to *B* and *B* to *A*
(c) *B* to *A*, *A* to *B* and *B* to *O*
(d) *A* to *B*

Matching Type

1 Match the statements given in column I with the suitable words given in column II:

Column I (*Statements*)	**Column II (*Words*)**
(a) A timing device based on simple pendulum	(i) Wall clock
(b) Time required to complete one oscillation	(ii) Sand clock
(c) Product of speed and time	(iii) Quartz clock
(d) A timing device based on balance wheel	(iv) 120 minute
(e) To and fro motion of pendulum	(v) Wrist watch
(f) Two hours is equals to	(vi) Distance
(g) Now-a-days clocks which have an electrical circuit	(vii) Oscillation
(h) A timing device which uses falling sand	(viii) Time period

Define the following terms:

1 Speed ____________________

2 Uniform motion ____________________

3 Periodic motion ____________________

Differentiate between the following:

1 Uniform and Non-uniform motion

____

2 Speed and Time

____

3 Circular motion and Rectilinear motion

____

Very Short Answer Type Questions

1 How can you say that motion of a child on a see-saw is an oscillatory motion?

2 In which unit, the speed of a fast moving object is commonly expressed?

3 Name the kind of watch used to measure time intervals during sports events.

4 Arrange in decreasing order: second, hour, minute, nanosecond

5 Choose odd one out and justify the correct choice:
Simple pendulum, bob, length of string, time period

6 Write one use of speedometer in the vehicles.

Short Answer Type Questions

1 Can you explain the most convenient way to find out which of the two objects is moving faster?

2 When a pendulum is said to have completed one oscillation? What is the time taken to complete one oscillation?

3 What are the units of time that we use in everyday life?

Long Answer Type Questions

1 Explain the working of some time measuring devices before the pendulum discovered.

2 Explain the different positions of a simple pendulum while it oscillates with the help of diagram.

Worksheet 2 Distance-Time Graph

True/False

1 Write 'T' for True or 'F' for False for the following statements:

(a) A pie chart or a bar graph can't represent the uniform motion of a body. ☐

(b) The distance-time graph of a car moving with uniform speed is a curved line. ☐

(c) A straight line graph indicates equal distance covered in equal intervals of time. ☐

(d) Motion of a body can't be represented graphically. ☐

Fill in the Blanks

1 Fill in the blanks with the suitable words:

(a) The composition of air in our atmosphere can graphically be represented by ________.

(b) The plot of distance-time graph for a uniform motion is ________.

(c) The distance-time graph is a type of ________ graph.

Multiple Choice Questions (MCQs)

1 Which of the following option is correct regarding the motion of a body with constant speed?

(a) Its position remains constant as time passes

(b) It covers equal distance in unequal time intervals

(c) Its acceleration is zero

(d) It doesn't change its direction of motion

2 If an object is moving with constant velocity then which of the graphs shown below correctly represent it?

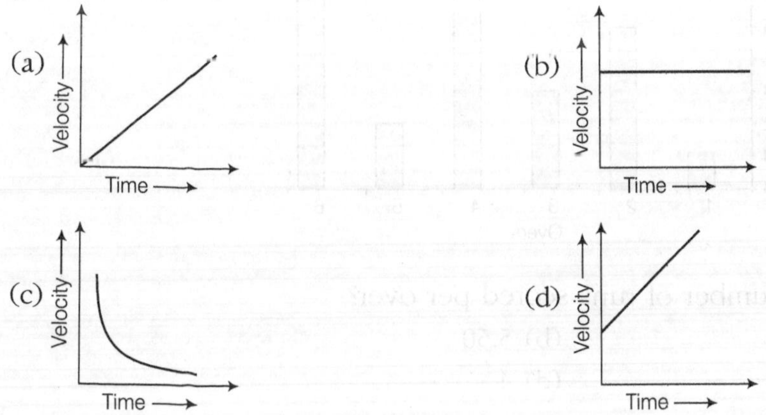

3 Two students were asked to plot a distance-time graph for the motion described by Table *A* and Table *B*.

Table *A*

Distance moved (m)	0	10	20	30	40	50
Time (minutes)	0	2	4	6	8	10

Table *B*

Distance moved (m)	0	5	10	15	20	25
Time (minutes)	0	1	2	3	4	5

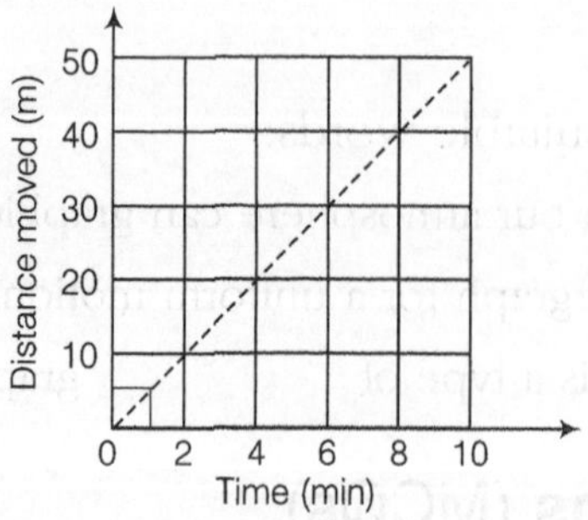

The graph given in the figure is true for

(a) Both *A* and *B* (b) Only *A*

(c) Only *B* (d) Neither *A* nor *B*

4 A bar graph given below is representing the number of runs scored in consecutive overs.

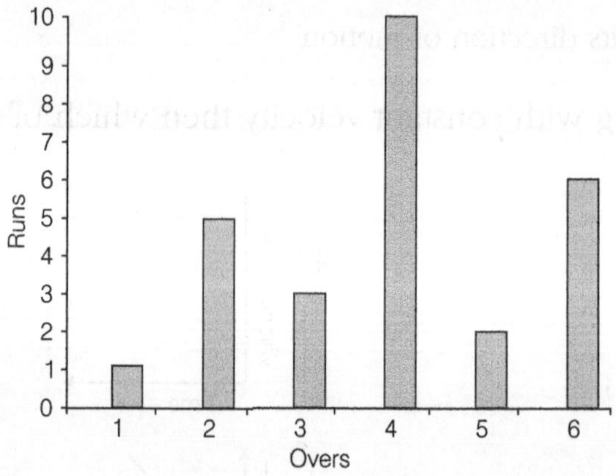

What are the average number of runs scored per over?

(a) 3.25 (b) 5.50

(c) 4.5 (d) 4

5 A bus travels 54 km in 90 minutes. The speed of the bus is

(a) 0.6 m/s (b) 10 m/s

(c) 5.4 m/s (d) 3.6 m/s

6 A track event at the school sports day is 1.5 km long. Satyam takes 5 min to cover it. The speed of Satyam is

(a) 30 km/min (b) 50 m/min (c) 0.3 km/min (d) 10 m/min

7 We know that light travels with the speed of 3×10^8 m/s and time required by light reaches from sun to earth is 8 second. How far is the sun from earth?

(a) 24×10^8 m (b) $\frac{3}{8} \times 10^8$ m

(c) $\frac{8}{3} \times 10^8$ m (d) None of these

8 A car is moving with a velocity of 20 m/s. After how much time, it will cover a distance of 100 m?

(a) 5 s (b) 5 min (c) 5 h (d) None of these

Define the following terms:

1 Pie chart ______________________

2 Bar graph ______________________

3 *X*-axis ______________________

4 *Y*-axis ______________________

Differentiate between the following:

1 Bar graph and Line graph

____

2 Distance-time graph and Speed-time graph

____

Very Short Answer Type Questions

1 Figure given below shows the distance-time graph of the two moving bodies. Which one of them is moving faster?

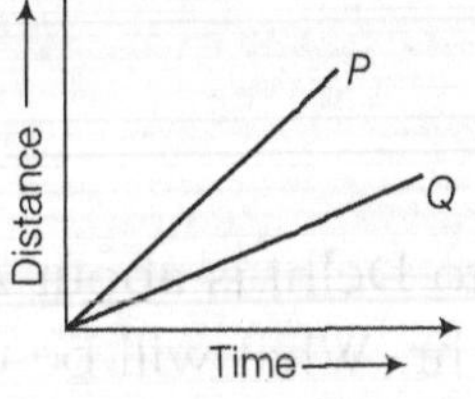

____

2 Give the nature of distance-time graph for the motion of an object moving with variable speed.

3 Give two points that should be kept in mind while plotting graph.

Short Answer Type Questions

1 A boy is running at the speed of 10 km/h. Find the distance travelled by him in 30 s.

2 Khushbu and Nitish have to cover different distances to reach their school but they take the same time to reach the school. What can you say about their speed?

3 Complete the data of the table given below with the help of the distance-time graph given in the figure.

Distance (m)	0	4	?	12	?	20
Time (s)	0	2	4	?	8	10

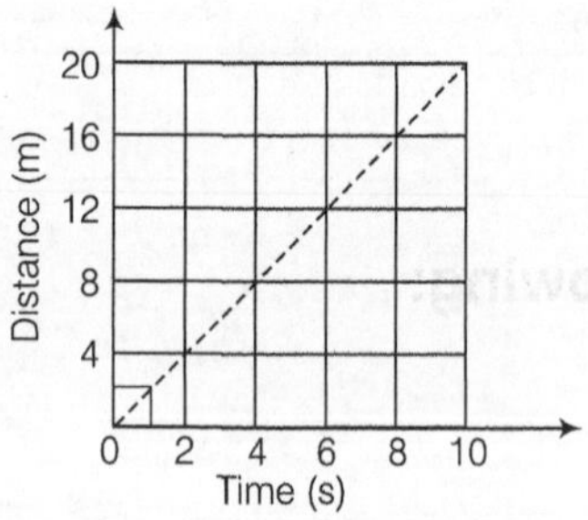

4 If Rahul covers a certain distance of 5 km in one hour and Sarita covers the same distance in two hours. Calculate their speed and tell, who travels with a higher speed?

5 A boy runs 200 m in 5 second, what is the speed of boy?

6 A helicopter is flying at a speed of 600 km/h. After how much time it covers a distance of 200 km?

7 The distance between Kolkata to Delhi is about 2000 km. A plane starts flying from Kolkata and reaches Delhi in 4 hr. What will be the speed of plane?

Long Answer Type Questions

1 Plot a distance-time graph of the tip of the second hand of a clock by selecting 4 points on *X*-axis and *Y*-axis, respectively. The circumference of the circle traced by the second hand is 64 cm.

2 A truck moves with a speed of 60 km/hr for 30 minutes. What is the total distance travelled by the truck? Also, show the distance-time graph for a truck moving with a constant speed.

SUMMATIVE ASSESSMENT

BASED ON COMPLETE CHAPTER .....

Multiple Choice Questions (MCQs) (1 mark each)

1 Given diagrams show movement of different bodies. Which of two have similar movement?

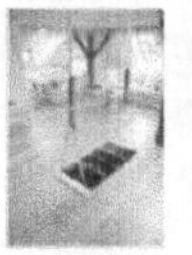
A

B

C

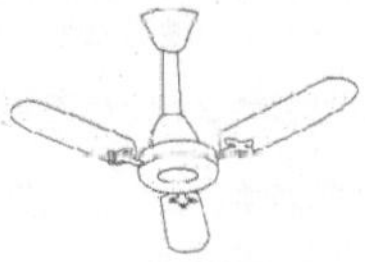
D

(a) *A* and *D* (b) *B* and *C* (c) *B* and *D* (d) None of these

2 Match the columns and choose the correct option given below:

A. Months	I m/s
B. Speed	II Second
C. Time	III Time from one sunrise to next
D. Day	IV One new moon to next

	A	B	C	D
(a)	IV	I	II	III
(b)	I	II	IV	III
(c)	II	I	IV	III
(d)	IV	I	III	II

3 Which of the following is not a unit of speed?

(a) Metre/second (b) Second/metre
(c) km/hour (d) km/minute

4 Choose the correct statement among the following:

(a) The basic unit of time is second.
(b) A child in a Ferris wheel undergoes translatory motion.
(c) Speed is the distance moved by an object.
(d) Buses and trucks move at uniform speed.

5 Time taken by the bob to move from A to C is t_1 and from C to O is t_2 as shown in the figure. The time period of this simple pendulum is

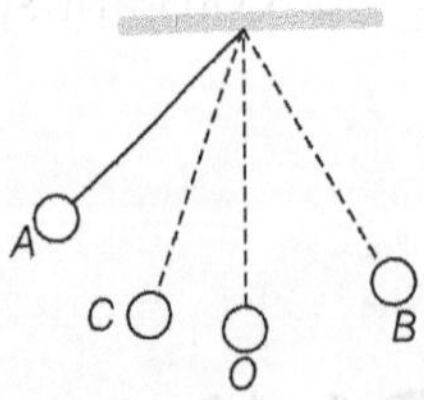

(a) $(t_1 + t_2)$ (b) $3(t_1 + t_2)$
(c) $2(t_1 + t_2)$ (d) $4(t_1 + t_2)$

Very Short Answer Type Questions (1 mark each)

1 How can we determine the motion made by anybody to be uniform or non-uniform?

2 Why do we need to measure time?

3 Shatabdi express takes 6 hours to reach Lucknow at a speed of 60 km/h. Find the distance it travels.

4 A spaceship travels 36,000 km in 1 hour. Express its speed in km/s.

5 The average age of children of class VIII is 12 years and 3 months. Express this age in seconds.

Short Answer Type I Questions (2 marks each)

1 By giving an example, show that rest and motion are relative terms.

2 What is the SI unit of speed? Give one more unit to measure speed.

Short Answer Type II Questions (3 marks each)

1 A simple pendulum is oscillating between two points A and B as shown in the figure. Is the motion of the bob uniform or non-uniform?

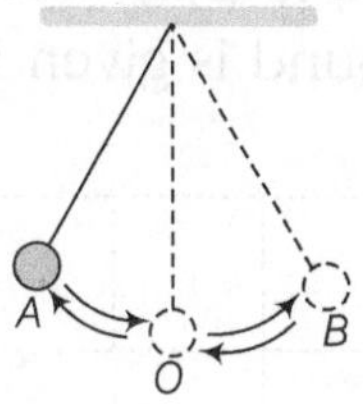

2 Starting from A, Paheli moves along a rectangular path $ABCD$ as shown in the figure. She takes 2 minutes to travel each side. Plot a distance-time graph and explain whether the motion is uniform or non-uniform.

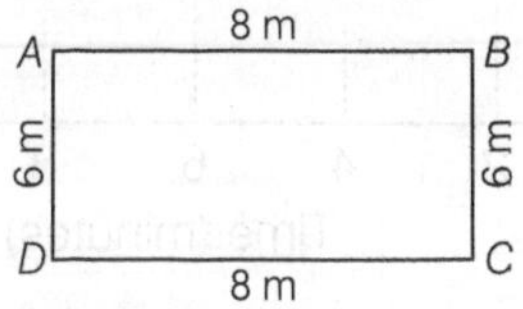

Long Answer Type Questions (5 marks each)

1 Distance between Bholu's and Golu's house is 9 km. Bholu has to attend Golu's birthday party at 7 o'clock. He started from his home at 6 o'clock on his bicycle and covered a distance of 6 km in 40 minutes. At that point, he met Chintu and he spoke to him for 5 minutes and reached Golu's birthday party at 7 o'clock. With what speed did he cover the second part of the journey? Calculate his average speed for the entire journey.

2 Given below is a figure representing the distance-time graph of motion of an object.

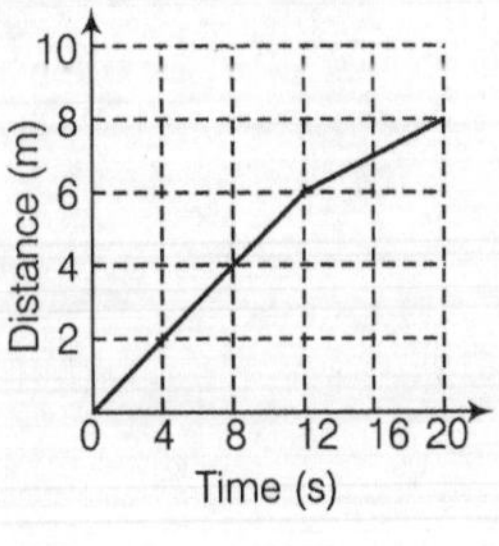

(a) What will be the position of the object at 20 s?

(b) What will be the distance travelled by the object in 12 s?

(c) What is the average speed of the object?

ACTIVITY (Graph Plotting)

1 Raghu goes to the football ground to play football. The distance-time graph of his journey from his home to the ground is given in the figure below:

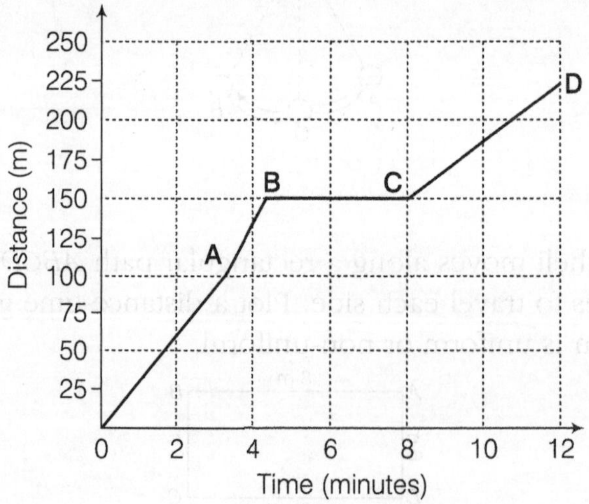

What does the graph between point *B* and *C* indicates about the motion of Raghu?

Chapter 14

Electric Current and Its Effect

Worksheet 1 Electric Circuit and Its Components

Fill in the Blanks

1 Fill in the blanks with the suitable words:

(a) An electric cell has __________ and __________ terminals.

(b) The batteries used in tractors, trucks and inverters are made up of __________.

(c) In the bulb, there is a thin wire called __________.

(d) If the filament of the bulb is broken, the bulb will not __________ as the electric circuit is __________.

(e) The __________ is used to connect the various electrical components in a circuit.

True/False

1 Write 'T' for True or 'F' for False for the following statements:

(a) A longer line of electric cell represents positive terminal. ☐

(b) It is good to represent electric components by its symbols. ☐

(c) To make a battery, the negative terminal of a cell is connected with positive terminal of other cell. ☐

(d) Torches, transistors, etc does not use electric cell. ☐

(e) A connecting wire in the electric circuit is represented by *zig-zag* line. ☐

Multiple Choice Questions (MCQs)

1 A device used to open and close electric circuit is

(a) fuse (b) wire (c) switch (d) resistance

2 When a switch is in 'OFF' position?

(a) Circuit is close (b) Circuit is open (c) Bulb glows (d) None of these

3 Which of the following is not a circuit element?

(a) Voltmeter (b) Resistor (c) Battery (d) Potential difference

4 Which of the following statement is true regarding the given circuit diagram?

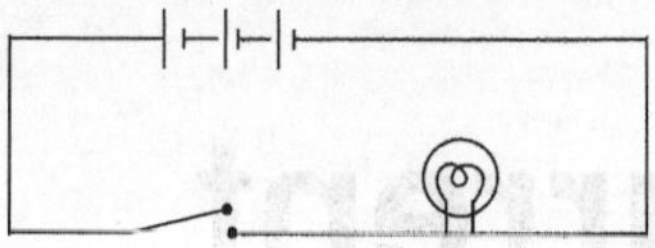

(a) It is a complete circuit (b) The bulb will not glow

(c) The wire is broken (d) Electric current flows wrong way

5 Which of the following option is incorrect?

(a) Light, fans, computers should be switched 'OFF' when not needed.

(b) We should use low electricity consuming devices.

(c) We must install wind mills and solar cells for electrical energy.

(d) A solar cell converts sound energy into electrical energy.

Matching Type

1 Match the words given in column I with the suitable symbols given in column II:

Column I (*Words*)	Column II (*Symbols*)
(a) Connecting wire	(i) 
(b) Switch 'ON' position	(ii) 
(c) Electric cell	(iii) 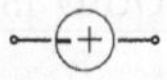
(d) Electric bulb	(iv) 
(e) Switch 'OFF' position	(v) 
(f) Battery	(vi) 
(g) Resistance	(vii) 
(h) Voltage source	(viii) 

Define the following terms:

1 Cell holder

2 Battery

Differentiate between the following:

1 Cell and Battery

2 Open circuit and Closed circuit

Very Short Answer Type Questions

1 How an electric bulb glows when an electric current is switched ON?

2 What do you mean by an electric circuit?

3 Satyam made an electric circuit using a cell holder (as shown in the figure given below), a switch and a bulb. When he put the switch in the ON position, the bulb did not glow. Identify the possible defects in the circuit.

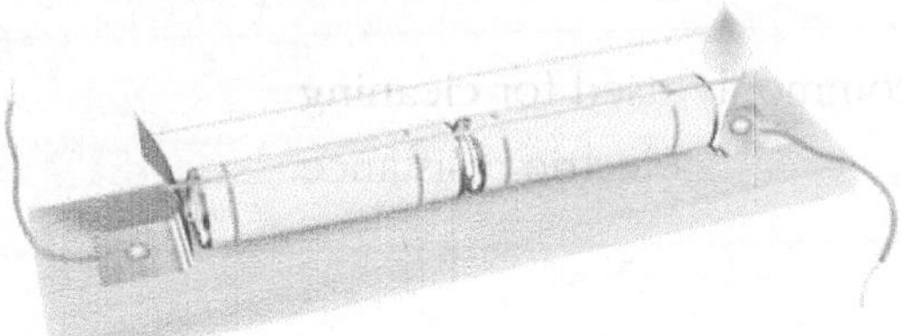

4 Choose odd one out and justify the correct choice:

cell, battery, cell holder, electric bulb

Short Answer Type Questions

1 Why should not we touch a lighted electric bulb?

2 "Don't experiment with the electric supply from mains". Justify the given statement.

3 Which part of the symbol of battery shows positive and negative terminals?

Long Answer Type Question

1 Draw a circuit diagram containing each components of electrical circuit. Describe function of each component of it.

Worksheet 2 Effects of Electric Current

Fill in the Blanks

1 Fill in the blanks with the suitable words:

(a) The electric current passing through a wire can produce ________ and ________ effect.

(b) A coil of wire present in room heater or an electric heater is called ________.

(c) The amount of heat produced in a wire depends on its ________, ________ and ________.

(d) The ________ reduce the wastage of electric current and can be fixed in the ordinary bulb holders.

(e) The steel wool is commonly used for cleaning ________.

(f) A fuse wire has ________ electric resistance.

True/False

1 Write 'T' for True or 'F' for False for the following statements:

(a) An electric current passing through any conductor produces heat. ☐

(b) The coiled wire in an electrical heating devices called compound. ☐

(c) The electric fuse is a wire which prevents short circuit. ☐

(d) Different fuses should be used for different devices to prevent short circuit. ☐

(e) Nichrome is an alloy of nickel and chromium. ☐

Matching Type

1 Match the statements given in column I with the suitable words given in column II:

Column I (*Statements*)	**Column II** (*Words*)
(a) Coiled wire of an electric heater	(i) Permanent magnet
(b) An alloy used as fuse wire	(ii) Element
(c) Sound producing device works on the principle of electromagnet	(iii) Christian Oersted
(d) A material used to make an electromagnet	(iv) Fusible alloy
(e) An instrument used to measure current	(v) Tungsten
(f) A device used to find direction	(vi) Electric bell
(g) Excess current in electric circuit cause damage of device	(vii) Ammeter
(h) An alloy of 60% nickel, 25% iron and 15% chromium	(viii) Magnetic compass
(i) Long and thin filament of bulb is made up of	(ix) Short circuit
(j) Magnetic effect of current is discovered by	(x) Nichrome
(k) A material which doesn't lose its magnetism when electric current stops	(xi) Soft iron

Multiple Choice Questions (MCQs)

1 The element of electric iron is made up of

(a) nichrome (b) copper

(c) iron (d) tungsten

2 Which of the following device doesn't use an electromagnet?

(a) Washing machine (b) Refrigerator

(c) Electric iron (d) Electric bell

3 The condition for a fuse wire is

(a) conductor with low melting point (b) insulator with low melting point

(c) conductor with high melting point (d) insulator with high melting point

4 During the time of short circuit, the current in the circuit

(a) doesn't change (b) reduces

(c) increases rapidly (d) varies

5 Choose the correct option for the given labelling of the figure.

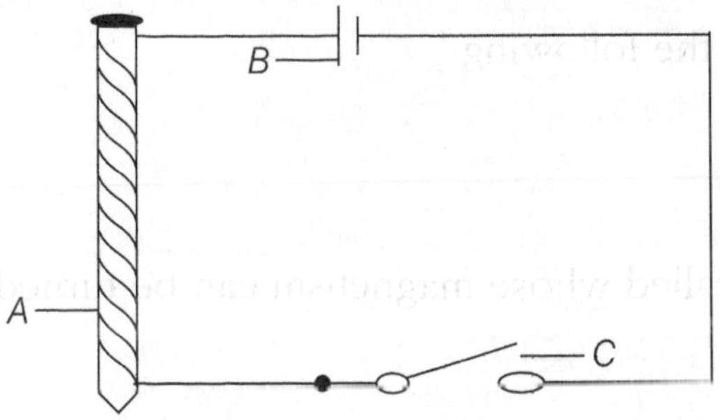

(a) *A*-Electromagnet *B*-Switch *C*-Battery/Cell

(b) *A*-Switch *B*-Battery/Cell *C*-Electromagnet

(c) *A*-Switch *B*-Electromagnet *C*-Battery/Cell

(d) *A*-Electromagnet *B* Battery/Cell *C*-Switch

6 When a magnetic compass is brought near a current carrying wire

(a) it loses its magnetism (b) magnetic needle is deflected

(c) no effect on the magnetic needle (d) None of these

Define the following terms:

1 Electric fuse

2 Electromagnet

Give reasons for the following:

1 The magnetic needle moves when electric current is passed through nearby wire.

2 CFLs should be used in place of bulbs.

Very Short Answer Type Questions

1 Which effect of electric current is used
(a) in an electric bell?

(b) in an electric iron?

2 Name the device which is used in place of electric fuses.

3 Give the full form of the following:
(a) MCB
(b) ISI

4 What is the magnet called whose magnetism can be turned 'ON' or 'OFF'?

5 Choose odd one out and justify the correct choice:
(a) Electric bell, electric kettle, electric bulb, electric iron

(b) Washing machine, electric fan, electric bell, electric heater

6 Differentiate between heating effect of current and magnetic effect of current.

Short Answer Type Questions

1 Give the dependence of amount of heat produced in a wire when electric current is passed through it.

2 Give two characteristics of a fuse wire.

3 Briefly explain, how does fuse wire protect an electric circuit?

4 What happens when a bulb gets fused?

5 An electrician working in your home wants to replace a blown up fuse wire with a piece of copper wire. Would you agree? Give reason for your answer.

Long Answer Type Questions

1 Your teacher has shown you the following activity.

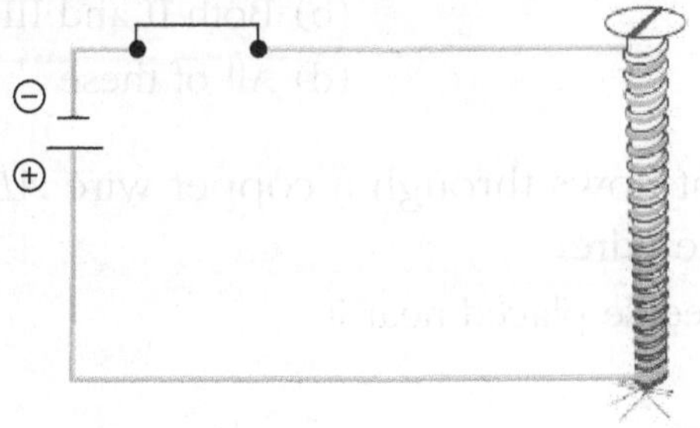

Activity Teacher has wound a long insulated piece of wire around an iron nail in the form of a coil. Free ends of the wire are connected to a cell through a switch as shown in the figure. The current is switched ON and some pins are placed near the ends of the nail.

(a) What happens when some pins are brought close to the end of the nail?

(b) What happens to the pins when the current is switched 'OFF'?

(c) What is the name given to such type of coils?

2 Explain with the help of a diagram, how does the magnetic effect of current help in the working of an electric bell?

SUMMATIVE ASSESSMENT

BASED ON COMPLETE CHAPTER .....

Multiple Choice Questions (MCQs) (1 mark each)

1 When a switch is in 'OFF' position,

I. circuit starting from the positive terminal of the cell stops at the switch.

II. circuit is open.

III. no current flows through it.

IV. current flows after some time.

Choose the combination of correct answer from the following:

(a) Both I and II (b) Both II and III

(c) Only IV (d) All of these

2 When an electric current flows through a copper wire *AB* as shown in the figure. The wire

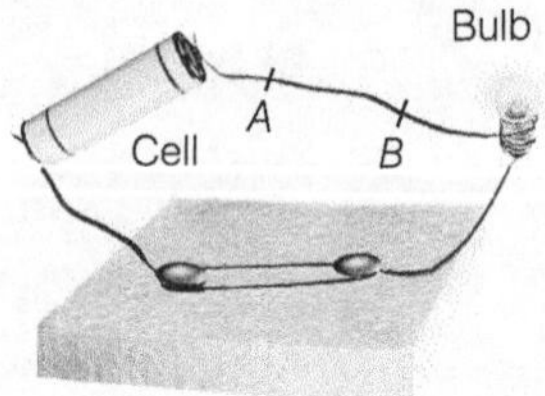

(a) deflects a magnetic needle placed near it

(b) becomes red hot

(c) give electric shock

(d) behaves like a fuse

3 Three bulbs *A*, *B* and *C* are connected in a circuit as shown below. When the switch is 'ON',

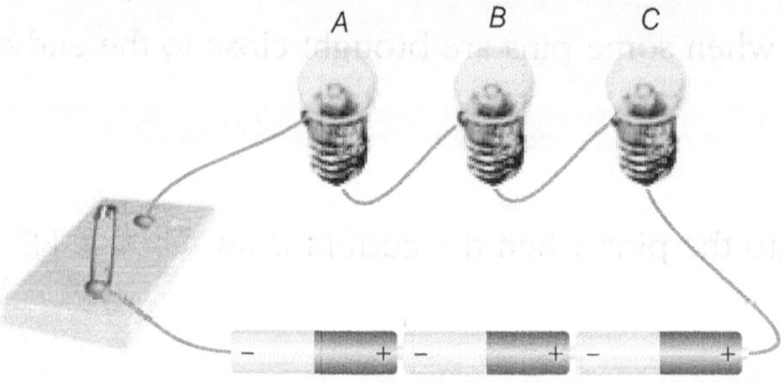

(a) bulb *C* will glow first

(b) bulb *B* and *C* will glow simultaneously and bulb *A* will glow after some time

(c) all the bulbs *A*, *B* and *C* will glow at the same time

(d) the bulbs will glow in the order *A*, *B* and *C*

4 Which of the following does not work on the heating effect of electric current?

(a) Electric bulb (b) MCB

(c) Electric bell (d) Immersion rod

5 Choose the correct match from the following.

A. Cell	(i) Secondary source
B. Generator	(ii) Insulator
C. Fuse	(iii) Primary source
D. Rubber	(iv) Safety device

(a) A - (i), B - (iii), C - (iv), D - (ii)
(b) A - (iii), B - (iv), C - (ii), D - (i)
(c) A - (iii), B - (i), C - (iv), D - (ii)
(d) A - (i), B - (iii), C - (ii), D - (iv)

Very Short Answer Type Questions (1 mark each)

1 What name is given to the following arrangement?
A wire of insulated copper wrapped over iron piece.

2 Which property of conducting wire is utilised in making fuse?

3 Who invented the electric bulb?

4 Choose odd one out and justify the correct choice:
(a) Dry cell, electric bulb, solar cell, wet cell

(b) Electric motors, electric bells, electric toaster, telephones

5 Why is an electric fuse required in all electrical appliances?

Short Answer Type I Questions (2 marks each)

1 Can we use the same fuse in a geyser and a television set? Explain.

2 Why do we cover plug pin holes which are within the reach of children with cellotape or a plastic cover when not in use?

Short Answer Type II Questions (3 marks each)

1 Arun doesn't have a night lamp in his room. In order to get dim light in the night, he covered the bulb of his room with a dry cloth. State whether he has taken the right step or not? Give one reason to justify your answer.

2 Shyam made an electromagnet by winding 50 turns of wire over an iron screw. Radha also made an electromagnet by winding 100 turns over a similar iron screw. Which electromagnet will attract more pins? Give reason.

____

Long Answer Type Questions (5 marks each)

1 Write a brief note on the terms "Short Circuit" and "Overloading". Mention two causes, why do current exceeds in overloading?

____

____

2 Describe how can you make an electromagnet in a laboratory. Also, give some examples and applications of electromagnet.

____

____

ACTIVITY 1 (Crossword)

Complete the crossword with the help of clues given below:

Across

1 A coil which behave as a magnet when current is supplied to it.

3 When an electric current flows through a wire, it behaves like a ____.

5 When the filament of a bulb is broken, the bulb is called _____.

6 It is convenient to represent electric component by _____.

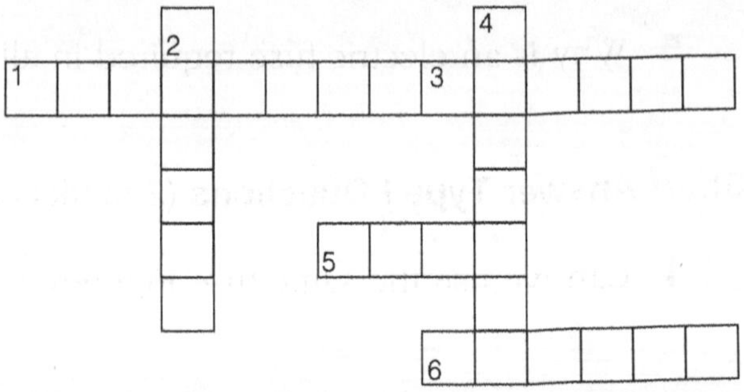

Down

2 When an electric current flows through a wire, the wire gets _____.

4 This is the combination of two or more cells.

Chapter 15

Light

Worksheet 1 Reflection of Light

True/False

1 Write 'T' for True or 'F' for False for the following statements:

(a) Light rays always travel in straight line. ☐

(b) An object can be seen only if it emits light. ☐

(c) The inner surface of steel spoon acts as a concave mirror. ☐

(d) A convex mirror is also known as diverging mirror. ☐

(e) The image formed by concave mirror is always behind the mirror. ☐

(f) A real image can't be taken on screen. ☐

(g) A virtual image is always erect. ☐

Fill in the Blanks

1 Fill in the blanks with the suitable words:

(a) Light is a form of ________.

(b) The image formed by ________ is erect, virtual and of same size as that of object.

(c) Any polished or a shining surface acts as a ________.

(d) A concave mirror can form ________ and ________ image.

(e) A convex mirror always forms a ________, ________ and diminished image.

(f) ________ image can be obtained on the screen.

(g) The image which can't be obtained on screen is called ________ image.

Matching Type

1 Match the statements given in column I with the suitable words given in column II:

Column I (*Statement*)	Column II (*Word*)
(a) Mirror mainly used as looking glasses	(i) Concave
(b) Propagation of light in straight line	(ii) Plane mirror
(c) Image smaller than object	(iii) Convex
(d) A concave mirror is also called	(iv) Rectilinear
(e) Mirror used as side mirror in car	(v) Converging mirror
(f) Mirror used by dentists to see enlarged image	(vi) Diminished image

Multiple Choice Questions (MCQs)

1 In the case of reflection

(a) virtual image is on the same side as the object

(b) real image is on the other side of the reflector

(c) Both virtual and real images are on the same side as the object

(d) None of the above

2 If we look at our image in a plane mirror, we see

(a) our right hand is on the right side of the mirror

(b) our image is upside down

(c) our left hand is on the left hand side

(d) our right hand is on the left side of the mirror

3 The image of the teeth seen by a dentist while testing teeth is

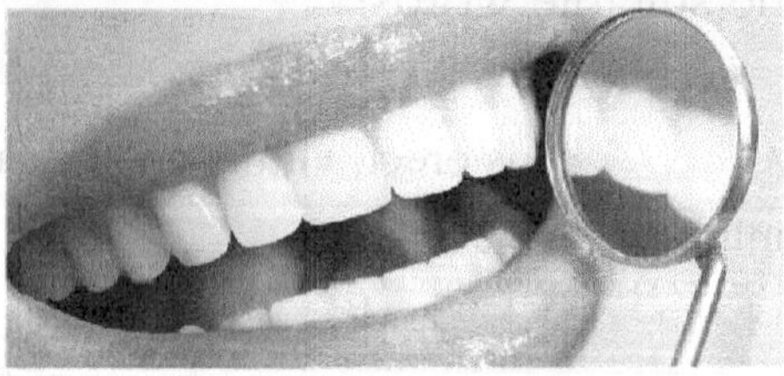

(a) Erect and real
(b) Erect and virtual
(c) Inverted and virtual
(d) Inverted and real

4 Why is word 'AMBULANCE' written right to left and inverted?

(a) To get everyone's attention.

(b) Because the ambulance driver can read it easily from his seat

(c) Because the drivers of the vehicle's ahead it sees a laterally inverted image of the word 'AMBULANCE' in their rear view mirrors.

(d) None of the above

5 Which of the following is a concave mirror?

(a)

(b)

(c)

(d) Both (a) and (b)

6 You are provided with a concave mirror, a convex mirror, a concave lens and a convex lens. To obtain an enlarged image of an object, you can use either

(a) concave mirror or convex mirror
(b) concave mirror or convex lens
(c) concave mirror or concave lens
(d) concave lens or convex lens

7 If the image formed is always virtual, the mirror can be

(a) concave or convex
(b) concave or plane
(c) convex or plane
(d) only convex

Define the following terms:

1 Reflection

---

2 Plane mirror

Give reasons for the following:

1 Image in the mirror are closer than they appear is written on the rear view mirror of vehicle.

---

2 Convex mirrors used as side mirrors in automobiles.

---

3 Dentist uses concave mirror to investigate tooth.

Differentiate between the following:

1 Concave mirror and Convex mirror

---

2 Real image and Virtual image

Very Short Answer Type Questions

1 Which phenomena of light is involved in the formation of image by convex mirror?

2 Name any two letters of English alphabet in which image formed in a plane mirror appears exactly same.

3 If the distance between the object and the plane mirror is 10 cm, then what will be the distance between the object and its image?

4 What is the shape of the 'dish' of a dish antenna used for receiving TV signals?

5 What type of mirror is the

(a) rear view mirror of vehicle.

(b) back-side surface of shining steel spoon.

(c) front-side surface of shining steel spoon.

Short Answer Type Questions

1 The concave reflecting surface of a torch got rusted. What effect would this have on the beam of light from the torch?

2 The side mirror of a scooter got broken. The mechanic replaced it with a plane mirror. Mention any inconvenience that the driver of the scooter will face while using it?

3 An erect and enlarged image of an object is formed on a screen. Explain, how this could be possible?

4 What is the reason of using concave mirror as a reflector in headlights of a car?

5 You are given three mirrors of different types, how will you identify the type of each one of them?

____

Long Answer Type Questions

1 Explain the properties of image formed in a plane mirror?

____

____

2 Explain how we are able to see an object placed on the table though it doesn't give out its own light?

____

____

Worksheet 2 Refraction of Light

True/False

1 Write 'T' for True or 'F' for False for the following statements:

(a) Bending of a ray of light on passing through a medium is called refraction. ☐

(b) A concave lens generally converges all light rays. ☐

(c) It is good to look through a lens at the sun or a bright light. ☐

(d) Rainbow is an example of dispersion of light. ☐

(e) A white light passing through a lens split into different colours. ☐

(f) A white light consists of 8 colours. ☐

Fill in the Blanks

1 Fill in the blanks with the suitable words:

(a) The image of concave lens is always ________ than the object.

(b) A concave lens ________ parallel rays, whereas a convex lens ________ parallel rays of light.

(c) A magnifying glass and reading glass have ________ lenses.

(d) Parallel rays of light when passed through convex lens converges at a point called ________.

(e) Image formed by concave lens is always ________.

(f) When object is placed very close to a convex lens, the image formed will be ________.

(g) When a disc painted with the seven colours of rainbow is rotated rapidly, it appears to be ________.

Matching Type

1 Match the words given in column I with the statements given in column II:

Column I (*Words*)	Column II (*Statements*)
(a) Convex lens	(i) Mixture of seven colours
(b) White light	(ii) Can form both real and virtual images
(c) Prism	(iii) Object at very large distance
(d) Virtual image	(iv) A triangular glass splits white light
(e) Point size image	(v) Image formed by concave lens

Multiple Choice Questions (MCQs)

1 A virtual image larger than the object is produced by

(a) concave lens (b) convex lens

(c) plane mirror (d) convex mirror

2 When an object is kept at any distance in front of a concave lens, the image formed is always

(a) erect, virtual, magnified (b) erect, virtual, diminished

(c) erect, real, magnified (d) inverted, virtual, magnified

3 An image formed by a lens is erect. Such an image could be formed by a

(a) convex lens provided the image is smaller than object

(b) concave lens provided the image is smaller than object

(c) concave lens provided the image is larger than object

(d) concave lens provided the image is of the same size

4 A convex lens has a focal length of 5 cm. At which distance object should be placed so that it acts like a magnifying glass?

(a) At a distance less than 5 cm

(b) At a distance greater than 5 cm

(c) At a distance of 15 cm

(d) None of the above

Define the following terms:

1 Dispersion

2 Rainbow

Differentiate between the following:

1 Concave lens and Convex lens

2 Mirror and Lens

Very Short Answer Type Questions

1 Name the lens which can converge Sun's rays to a point and burn a piece of paper.

2 The image formed by a lens is always virtual, erect and smaller in size for an object kept at different positions in front of it. Identify the nature of the lens.

3 Where should an object be placed so that the convex lens works as a magnifying glass?

4 Satyam made light from a laser torch to fall on a prism. Will he be able to observe a band of seven colours? Why or why not?

Short Answer Type Questions

1 Give two important uses of concave lens?

2 Compare the image formed in case of concave and convex lens.

3 The distance between an object and a convex lens is changing. It is noticed that the size of the image formed on a screen is decreasing. Is the object moving in a direction towards the lens or away from it?

4 State the correct sequence (1-7) of colours in the spectrum formed by the prisms *A* and *B* as shown in the figure.

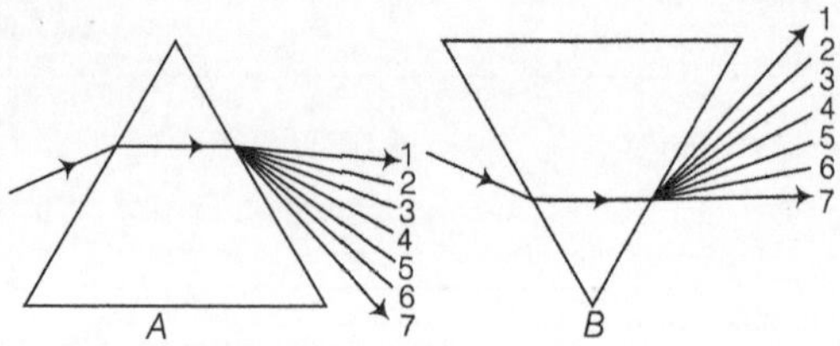

Long Answer Type Questions

1 Suppose we wish to obtain the real image of a distant tree. Explain two possible ways in which we can do it.

2 Explain with diagram how rainbow is formed after heavy rain?

SUMMATIVE ASSESSMENT

BASED ON COMPLETE CHAPTER .....

Multiple Choice Questions (MCQs) (1 mark each)

1 Which of the following statement is correct?

(a) Plane mirrors are used in microscopes

(b) The image is inverted in a plane mirror

(c) The distance of the object from the mirror is equal to the distance of image from the mirror

(d) If the object is 5 ft tall, the image in the plane mirror is $2\frac{1}{2}$ ft tall

2 What does the following figure depicts?

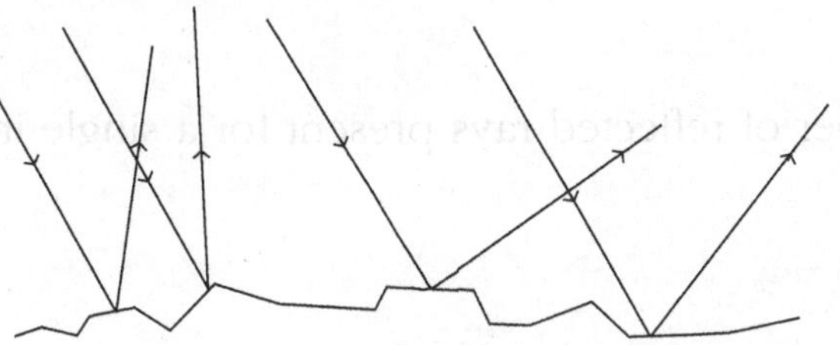

(a) Regular reflection
(b) Diffused reflection
(c) Refraction
(d) None of these

3 Sahil stood 3 m away from a plane mirror. He then moved 1 m away. Now the distance between him and the image is

(a) 4 m (b) 8 m (c) 6 m (d) 3 m

4 You are provided with a convex mirror, a concave mirror, a convex lens and a concave lens. You can get an inverted image from

(a) both concave lens and convex lens
(b) both concave mirror and convex mirror
(c) both concave mirror and convex lens
(d) both convex mirror and concave lens

5 Consider the diagram below. A wall separated Ajit from a ball but he was still able to see it.

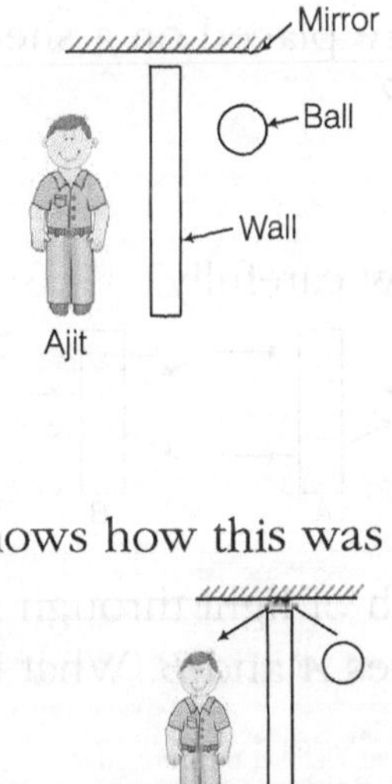

Which one of the following shows how this was possible?

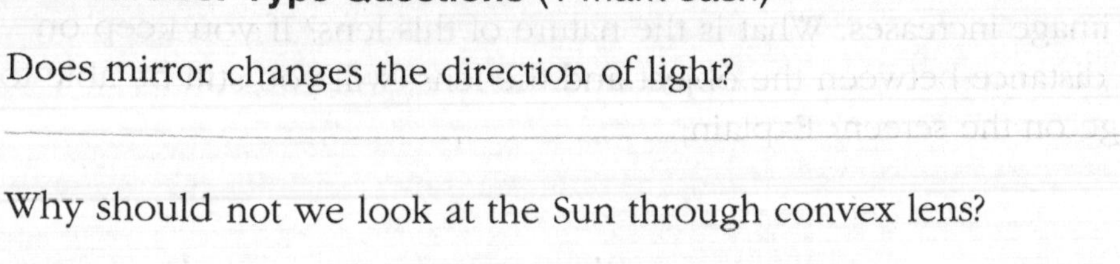

Very Short Answer Type Questions (1 mark each)

1 Does mirror changes the direction of light?

2 Why should not we look at the Sun through convex lens?

3 Why does the dispersion of light occur?

4 Mention the number of reflected rays present for a single incident ray in respect of a plane mirror.

5 Name the type of mirrors used by doctors for examining the eyes, ears, etc.

Short Answer Type I Questions (2 marks each)

1 In a truck mirror, the image of head appears much smaller than that of mouth. Explain why?

2 An erect and enlarged image of an object is formed on a screen. Explain how this could be possible?

Short Answer Type II Questions (3 marks each)

1 Two different types of lenses are placed on a sheet of newspaper. How will you identify them without touching?

2 Observe the figures given below carefully.

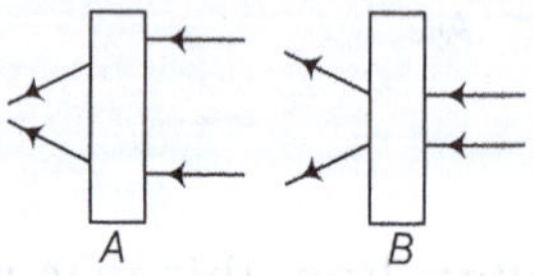

The given figures show the path of light through lenses of two different types, represented by rectangular boxes *A* and *B*. What is the nature of lenses *A* and *B*?

Long Answer Type Questions (5 marks each)

1 It was observed that when the distance between an object and a lens decreases, the size of the image increases. What is the nature of this lens? If you keep on decreasing the distance between the object and the lens, will you still be able to obtain the image on the screen? Explain.

2 (a) Explain the formation of rainbow in the sky.

(b) What do you mean by spectrum? Name the colours of spectrum in their order.

(c) Draw a diagram to show the dispersion of white light.

ACTIVITY (Word Identification)

Complete the following words:

(a) L _ _ _ _

Hint : This is a form of electromagnetic radiation which produces in our eyes the sensation of vision.

(b) _ I _ _ O _

Hint : A highly polished surface which is smooth enough to reflect a good fraction of light incident on it.

(c) L _ _ _

Hint : A piece of refracting medium bounded by two surfaces, at least one of which is curved surface.

(d) D _ _ E _ _ _ _ N

Hint : This is the phenomenon of splitting of white light into its component colours on passing through a refracting medium.

Chapter 16

Water : A Precious Resource

Worksheet 1 Sources and Forms of Water

Multiple Choice Questions (MCQs)

1 On which of the following day World Water Day is observed?
(a) 22 March (b) 14 November
(c) 2 October (d) 21 December

2 The minimum amount of water recommended by the United Nations per person per day is
(a) 25 L (b) 50 L (c) 75 L (d) 40 L

3 Groundwater will not be depleted due to
(a) thermal power plants (b) loss of forests and decreased rainfall
(c) afforestation (d) cropping of high water demanding crops

4 "Every Drop Counts" is a slogan related to
(a) counting of drops of any liquid (b) counting of water drops
(c) importance of water (d) importance of counting

5 Water exists in nature as
(a) solid only (b) liquid only
(c) solid and liquid (d) solid, liquid and gas

True/False

1 Write 'T' for True or 'F' for False for the following statements:
(a) Year 2003 was observed as the International year of freshwater. ☐
(b) Water drawn from under the ground gets replenished by seepage of rainwater. ☐
(c) Water in the aquifers can be pumped out with the help of tubewells or handpumps. ☐
(d) Ice is solid whereas snow is the semi-solid form of water. ☐
(e) The saline water present in the seas, oceans and partly as groundwater is not fit for human use. ☐

Matching Type

1 Match the items of column I with column II:

Column I	Column II
(a) Topmost level of underground water	(i) Groundwater
(b) Main source of water in India	(ii) Surface water
(c) Water present on the surface of the earth	(iii) Water table
(d) Water present inside the earth	(iv) Rainwater

Fill in the Blanks

1 Figure shows the processes involved in the water cycle. They are indicated by letters. Write the appropriate words for the letters given in the box:

evaporation	*transpiration*	*precipitation*	*infiltration*
groundwater	*condensation*	*clouds*	

Water Cycle

2 Fill in the blanks with the appropriate words:

(a) Building __________ on fast flowing rivers controls floods.

(b) The scarcity of water results in a condition called __________.

(c) Excess of rains can cause __________.

(d) The water in rivers and lakes comes from __________ and __________ of snow.

(e) In India, majority of farmers depend upon __________ for irrigating their __________.

Define the following terms:

1 Aquifer ____________________

2 Infiltration ____________________

3 Water table ____________________

4 Groundwater ____________________

Give reasons for the following:

1 Water is very important in sustaining life.

____

2 Increasing population is the main cause of the depletion of water table.

____

Very Short Answer Type Questions

1 What does the slogan *'Jal Hai to Kal Hai'* mean?

____

2 Name the two factors that cause the depletion of water table.

____

3 A list of jumbled words are given below. Write the correct form of each word:

(a) WASHFERRET ____________________

(b) CHARREGE ____________________

(c) QUIFERA ____________________

(d) WOSN ____________________

4 Give any two sources of water which are commonly used in urban areas.

____

Short Answer Type Questions

1 The diagram given below shows the changes in state that water goes through.

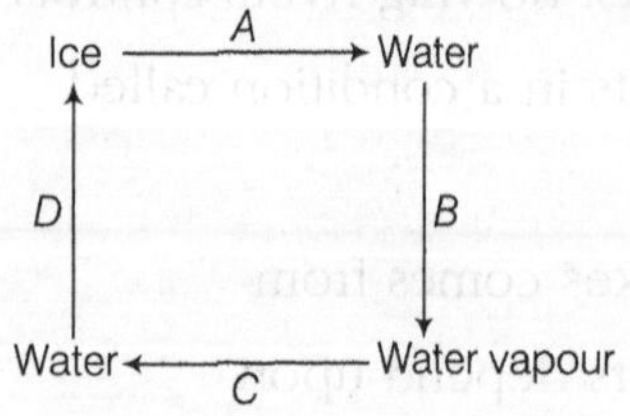

Which letter represents the following processes?

Condensation : ____________

Evaporation : ____________

Freezing : ____________

Melting : ____________

2 Explain how increasing industries and agricultural activities cause the depletion of water table?

____

Long Answer Type Question

1 Briefly describe the water cycle in nature.

____

____

Worksheet 2 Water Management

Multiple Choice Questions (MCQs)

1 Traditionally in India, structures called *bawris* were used for storing rainwater. The water collecting during monsoon was used during non-monsoon months. It was also used to recharge groundwater. Such type of water conservation is known as

(a) recycling water

(b) rainwater treatment

(c) rainwater harvesting

(d) drip irrigation

2 Check-dams were built on the river Rukmavati and its tributaries in Gujarat mainly to

(a) grow paddy crop

(b) recharge groundwater

(c) provide water to wild animals

(d) generate hydropower

3 There are various methods to conserve water like turn off taps while brushing or mop the floor instead of washing. Which of the methods given below does not result in water conservation?

(a) Recycling of water

(b) Planting more trees

(c) Using drip irrigation

(d) Cutting vegetation so that less water is lost by transpiration

Matching Type

1 Match the items of column I with column II:

Column I	Column II
(a) *Bawri*	(i) Wastage of water
(b) Drip irrigation	(ii) Rainwater harvesting
(c) Leaking taps	(iii) Small water tanks
(d) Recharging the groundwater	(iv) Water management

True/False

1 Write 'T' for True or 'F' for False for the following statements:

(a) Rainwater can be used to recharge the groundwater. ☐

(b) Water is not essential for all living beings. ☐

(c) Drip irrigation has a disadvantage that it is associated with huge loss of water. ☐

(d) Conservation of water means wise and judicious use of water. ☐

(e) The need of the hour is that every individual uses water economically. ☐

Fill in the Blanks

1 Complete the story with the appropriate words given in the box:

dry	*hot*	*scarcity*	*workers*	*harvesting*
rivers	*cold*	*lakes*	*storage*	

Rajasthan is a ____(a)____ and dry place. The challenge of natural ____(b)____ of water was met by a successful experiment. A band of social ____(c)____ had transformed a ____(d)____ area into a green place. They have revived five dried-up ____(e)____ by constructing water ____(f)____ structures.

2 Fill in the blanks with the suitable words:

(a) Leaking ________ is a source of huge water wastage.

(b) The best way to overcome shortage of water is ________.

(c) ________ check-dams were built on the Rukmavati river and its many tributaries.

Very Short Answer Type Questions

1 Name the traditional way of collecting water.

____

2 Name the technique of watering plants which minimises the wastage of water.

____

3 Name the ancient structures which are being revived now for water storage and water recharge in India.

4 What will happen if a plant is not watered for a few days?

Short Answer Type Question

1 Give some methods to conserve water at home and at school.

Long Answer Type Questions

1 Observe the figure given below and answer the following questions:

(a) Identify the figure.

(b) What is the importance of this process?

2 Why is the distribution of water over the globe not even?

SUMMATIVE ASSESSMENT

BASED ON COMPLETE CHAPTER .....

Multiple Choice Questions (MCQs) (1 mark each)

1 Which of the following does not show water shortage?
(a) Taps running dry
(b) Long queues for getting water
(c) Marches and protests for demand of water
(d) A family gets three buckets of water per person per day

2 Which of the following does not deplete the water table at a place?
(a) Increasing deforestation
(b) Scanty rainfall
(c) Increasing snowfall
(d) Increasing number of tube-wells

3 Which of the following sources of water is not used for drinking purpose due to dissolved salts present in them?
(a) Rainwater (b) Spring water (c) Sea water (d) River water

4 Which of the following inhibits the seepage of rainwater into ground?
(a) *Pakka* floor (b) Playground (c) Grass lawn (d) Forest land

5 Which of the following is a way to use water economically?
(a) Construction of *bawris*
(b) Rainwater harvesting
(c) Drip irrigation
(d) Infiltration

Very Short Answer Type Questions (1 mark each)

1 Why should we save water?

2 Why do certain regions on the earth become desert?

3 What is depletion of water table?

4 Define water cycle.

5 What are the main sources of underground water?

Short Answer Type I Questions (2 marks each)

1 List some ways how do groundwater helps plants/trees?

2 What does the phrase "shortage of water" mean?

Short Answer Type II Questions (3 marks each)

1 Place the following statements in a correct order to form a meaningful paragraph.

(a) Which in turn decreases the seepage of rainwater into the ground.

(b) This decreases the open areas like parks and playgrounds.

(c) Increasing population create demand for construction of houses, shops, roads, etc.

(d) This results in depletion of water table and creates scarcity of more water.

2 (a) Why does the earth appear blue from space?

(b) If there are eight tubewells in a lane of forty houses, what could be the long-term impact on the water table in the area?

(c) Choose the odd one out and justify the correct choice:

Evaporation, transpiration, condensation, clouds.

Long Answer Type Questions (5 marks each)

1 Describe the mismanagement of water at the level of water supply department and individual level.

2 Make a diagram showing groundwater and water table. Label its important parts.

ACTIVITY (Word Identification)

Complete the following words:

(a) The process which keeps the total amount of water on the earth constant.

__ __ __ __ __ __ __ __ __ L __

(b) The groundwater stored between layers of hard rock below the water table.

__ __ __ __ E __

(c) The area in Gujarat where check dams have been built

__ __ __ __ P __ __

(d) One of the five dried up river which has been revived in Rajasthan.

__ __ __ __ Z __ __ __ I

(e) A technique which water plants directly at their base

__ __ __ __ __ __ __ __ I __ __ T __ __ __

(f) An area in India where rainfall above 400 cm takes place

__ __ __ __ __ __ __ __ U __ __ I

Chapter 17

Forests : Our Lifeline

Multiple Choice Questions (MCQs)

1 On seeing children in the forest, some monkeys climbed higher up on the trees where they disturbed the birds. This is a type of

(a) natural behaviour of monkeys
(b) warning call to alert other animals
(c) angry nature of animals
(d) None of these

2 Understoreys formed in the forest are due to

(a) different heights of trees
(b) different types of crowns
(c) different sizes of crowns
(d) All of these

3 The functions of crowns of forest trees during the daytime are given.

I. Absorb sunlight energy
II. Absorb oxygen from air
III. Carry out photosynthesis
IV. Form a green cover

Choose the correct option:

(a) I and II
(b) II and III
(c) III and IV
(d) I, III and IV

4 Pick the option which gives the name of a tree and an animal respectively from the following:

(a) Semal, hornbill
(b) Sal, khair
(c) Chinkara, blue bull
(d) Neem, palash

5 Which type of organism is present at the first step in every food chain?

(a) Heterotroph
(b) Autotroph
(c) Saprotroph
(d) Scavenger

6 Which of the following shows correct arrangement in a food chain?

(a) Grass → Frog → Eagle → Insects → Snake
(b) Grass → Snake → Insects → Frog → Eagle
(c) Grass → Insects → Frog → Snake → Eagle
(d) Grass → Snake → Eagle → Insects → Frog

7 What will happen, if one component is removed from the forests?
(a) No change will take place
(b) Few other components would be affected
(c) All other components would be affected
(d) None of the above

8 One of the following is not produced by the action of decomposers on the dead parts of plants and dead bodies of animals. It is
(a) Carbon dioxide
(b) Oxygen
(c) Water
(d) Nutrients

Fill in the Blanks

1 Fill in the blanks with the appropriate words given in the bracket:
(a) Forests serve as green lungs and __________ (water purifying/air purifying) system of nature.
(b) The forests provide __________ (home/view) for many plants and animals.
(c) The layer of vegetation in a forest which is just below the understorey, is that of __________ (herbs/shrubs).
(d) __________ (Air/Soil) helps forests to grow and regenerate.
(e) If forests disappear, the amount of __________ (oxygen/carbon dioxide) in the air will increase.

2 Fill in the blanks given in the paragraph by using appropriate words from the box:

nutrients	*fungi*	*carbon dioxide*	*plants*
water	*bacteria*		

The organism ______(a)______ and ______(b)______ occur on the forest floor. They convert the dead parts of forest plants and dead bodies of forest animals into simple substances such as ______(c)______, ______(d)______ and ______(e)______ which can be re-used by ______(f)______ for their growth and development.

True/False

1 Write 'T' for True or 'F' for False for the following statements:
(a) Forests influence climate, water cycle and air quality. ☐
(b) In a forest, trees form the uppermost layer, followed by herbs. The shrubs form the lowest layer of vegetation. ☐
(c) The various components of the forest are interdependent on one another. ☐
(d) Plants release carbon dioxide in the process of photosynthesis. ☐
(e) Forests are the lifeline for the forest-dwelling communities. ☐

Matching Type

1 Match the terms of column I with column II:

Column I	Column II
(a) Decomposers	(i) Dead plants and animals
(b) Canopy	(ii) Habitats for wildlife
(c) Porcupine	(iii) Microorganisms
(d) Humus	(iv) Wild animal
(e) Forests	(v) Branches of tall trees

Define the following terms:

1 Understorey ______________________

2 Food chain ______________________

3 Humus ______________________

4 Photosynthesis ______________________

Give reasons for the following:

1 All the needs of animals living in a forest are fulfilled.

____

2 Nothing goes waste in a forest.

____

3 Forests serve as "green lungs".

____

4 We see a wide variety of trees in different forests.

____

Differentiate between the following:

1 Crown and Canopy

____

2 Deforestation and Regeneration

____

3 Decomposers and Autotrophs

____

Choose the odd one out and justify the correct choice:

1 Crow, jackal, lion, vulture

2 Gum, plywood, sealing wax, kerosene

3 Teak, sal, porcupine, kachnar

Very Short Answer Type Questions

1 Name the different layers of forest starting from top to bottom.

2 How can we recognise the presence of some animals in the forest?

3 Name the tree that provides us with

(a) medicines

(b) oil

(c) gum

(d) spices

Short Answer Type Questions

1 Give four examples of each:

(a) Useful products we get from forests.

(b) Commonly seen birds in a forest.

(c) Commonly seen animals in a forest.

(d) Commonly seen insects in a forest.

2 Explain how tribal people are able to live inside the forest.

3 What are the ways in which animals help forest to grow and regenerate?

4 Study the figure given below and answer the following questions based on it.

(a) The two processes taking place in the air.

(b) They slow down the speed of raindrops.

(c) They act as a sponge to absorb water.

(d) It helps water to seep down in the ground.

Long Answer Type Questions

1 Explain how the following functions are performed by the forests?

(a) Prevention of floods

(b) Prevention of soil erosion

(c) Cooling of climate

2 Describe the role of decomposers in a forest.

3 "Forests are our lifeline." Write five sentences to justify the statement.

4 The given figure shows a part of a forest.

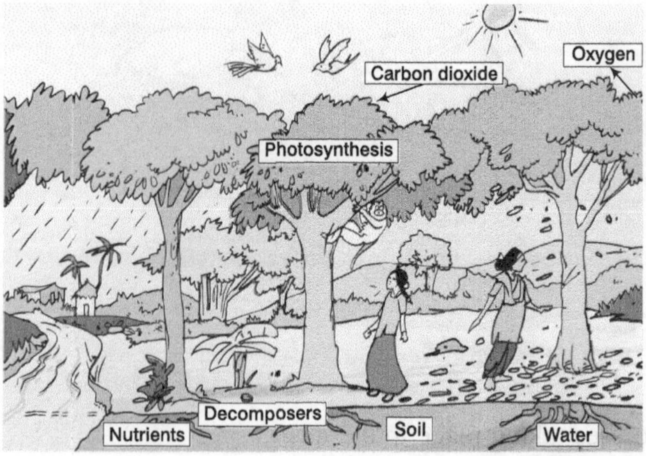

Write any five activities going on in the forest and their importance on the basis of this figure.

____

____

5 What are the causes and effects of cutting trees in a forest?

____

____

ACTIVITY (Word Identification)

Complete the following words:

(i) Planting of trees on large scale

_ _ _ _ _ _ _ _ T _ _ _ O _

(ii) The biotic community dominated by trees and spread over a large area.

_ _ _ _ _ T _

(iii) An overhanging covering like a roof over other plants in the forest.

_ _ _ _ P _

(iv) An animal which lives in the deeper areas of the forest.

_ _ _ O _

(v) A dark coloured organic substance formed by the decaying of plants and animals

_ _ _ _ S

[Chapter 18]

Wastewater Story

Worksheet 1 Treatment of Wastewater

Multiple Choice Questions (MCQs)

1 This logo to save water has been given by
(a) The General Assembly of the United Nations
(b) Indian National Congress
(c) United Nations Environment Programme
(d) United Nations Water Programme

WATER FOR LIFE
2005-2015

2 In a filtration plant, water is filtered using layers of
(a) sand and clay
(b) clay and fine gravel
(c) sand and fine gravel
(d) sand, fine gravel and medium gravel

3 Chlorination is done during wastewater treatment to
(a) clean the water in the beginning
(b) remove mud and dust particles only
(c) disinfect the water from microorganisms
(d) None of the above

True/False

1 Write 'T' for True or 'F' for False for the following statements:

(a) Cleaning of water is a process to remove the foul smell coming from water. ☐

(b) Generally in a city, manholes are located at every 2 km to 3 km in the sewerage. ☐

(c) A skimmer is used to remove the floatable solids like oil and grease. ☐

(d) Air is pumped into the clarified water to help aerobic bacteria to grow. ☐

(e) Treatment plants reduce pollutants in a wastewater up to a level where nature can take care of it. ☐

Fill in the Blanks

1 Fill in the blanks by using the appropriate words:

(a) Microbes other than bacteria may cause disease like ________.

(b) The process of wastewater treatment is commonly known as ________.

(c) The sludge gets decomposed by using ________ bacteria.

(d) The tank in which air is put into water is called ________.

(e) The activated sludge is about ________ water.

Matching Type

1 Match the type of sewage given in column I with their point of origin in column II and substance which contaminate it in column III:

Column I (*Type of Sewage*)	**Column II** (*Point of Origin*)	**Column III** (*Substance*)
(a) Sludge water	I. Toilets	(i) Human faeces, urine
(b) Foul waste	II. Kitchen	(ii) Nitrate, phosphates of metals
(c) Trade waste	III. Industrial and commercial organisations	(iii) Fruits and vegetable wastes, oil

Define the following terms:

1 Biogas ________

2 Aeration ________

3 Activated sludge ________

4 Contaminant ________

5 Sewage ________

Differentiate between the following:

1 Aerobic and Anaerobic bacteria

2 Wastewater and Pure water

Very Short Answer Type Questions

1 Expand the term WWTP.

2 Name three steps involved in the treatment of polluted water.

3 Can you name two chemicals which can be used to disinfect water?

4 Sewage is a complex mixture containing the following. Give two examples of each:

(a) Inorganic impurities

(b) Organic impurities

(c) Nutrients

(d) Bacterial diseases

Short Answer Type Questions

1 Discuss about the various sources of sewage.

2 What is done to sludge and clarified water in waste water treatment plant?

Long Answer Type Questions

1 The terms sewage, sewers and sewerage are interlinked with each other. Can you explain, how?

2 Write down some points about the international efforts undertaken/made to save water.

Worksheet 2 Sanitation and Diseases

Multiple Choice Questions (MCQs)

1 Sanitation can be best explained as

(a) the process of disposal of sewage and garbage from houses

(b) the process of making citizen responsible towards their own hygiene

(c) Both (a) and (b)

(d) None of the above

2 Ajay saw a same type of tree being planted all along the sewage pond. Which of the following tree would be that?

(a) *Ficus* tree (b) *Neem* tree (c) *Eucalyptus* tree (d) *Peepal* tree

3 If you are to organise an outdoor music festival in a park, which of the following toilet will you arrange?

(a) Composting toilets (b) Septic tank toilets

(c) Chemical toilets (d) None of these

4 Groundwater is a source of water for

(a) wells (b) tubewells (c) springs (d) All of these

True/False

1 Write 'T' for True or 'F' for False for the following statements:

(a) Cooking oils and fats should be thrown in a dustbin. ☐

(b) Contaminated drinking water is the only cause of a large number of diseases. ☐

(c) We should not defecate in open because untreated human excreta is a health hazard. ☐

(d) Vermi processing toilets use very less water for safe processing of human excreta. ☐

(e) As a good citizen, we should not follow the sanitation standards laid down by the government. ☐

Matching Type

1 Match the substances in column I with their effect of improper disposal in column II:

Column I	Column II
(a) Cooking oils and fats	(i) Kill helpful microbes
(b) Chemicals like paints	(ii) Hamper the degradation process
(c) Used tea leaves	(iii) Causes water and soil pollution
(d) Untreated human excreta	(iv) Harden and block the pipes

Very Short Answer Type Questions

1 Choose the odd one out and justify the correct choice:

(a) Paints, solvents, insecticides, oils

(b) Polio, hepatitis, dysentery, common cold

(c) Septic tanks, aeration tanks, chemical toilets, composting pits

2 Degradation process gets hampered in the drains due to non-availability of a gas. Which gas is it?

3 Name a suitable sewage disposal system for an isolated cluster of 4 or 5 houses in an area where there is no sewerage.

Short Answer Type Questions

1 Name any four water borne diseases which are caused by drinking contaminated water.

2 If a large amount of waste generated at public places is not disposed of properly then what will happen?

3 Open drains are not considered good for human health. Why?

Long Answer Type Questions

1 State the various ways in which you can contribute in maintaining sanitation at public places.

2 Write about three practices which should be practiced at our homes to minimise or eliminate waste at their source.

SUMMATIVE ASSESSMENT

BASED ON COMPLETE CHAPTER .....

Multiple Choice Questions (MCQs) (1 mark each)

1 Choose the correct sequence of treatment of polluted water.

(a) Aeration → chlorination → filtration

(b) Aeration → filtration → chlorination

(c) Filtration → aeration → chlorination

(d) Chlorination → aeration → filtration

2 The purpose of screening during WWTP is to

(a) remove large pieces of rubbish (b) remove sludge

(c) remove microorganisms (d) None of these

3 Water polluted by various human activities cause a number of water borne diseases. Which of the following is not a water borne disease?

(a) Cholera (b) Typhoid (c) Asthma (d) Dysentery

4 Which statements best describes the relationship between sanitation and disease?

I. Diseases are caused due to poor sanitation

II. Sanitation should be kept to avoid diseases

Choose the correct option:

(a) Only I (b) Only II (c) I and II (d) None of these

5 Which of the following is waste water?

(a) Water trickling from a damaged tap (b) Water coming out of a shower

(c) Water flowing in a river (d) Water coming out of a laundary

Very Short Answer Type Questions (1 mark each)

1 Name two things that can be made from sludge extracted during treatment of sewage.

2 What are sewers?

3 What purpose do microorganisms serve in sewage treatment?

4 What type of toilets are used in aeroplanes?

5 Which type of a toilet is most likely to contaminate water of a handpump installed nearby?

Short Answer Type I Questions (2 marks each)

1 Write the various uses of water in our life.

2 "Sanitation and diseases are interrelated". How?

Short Answer Type II Questions (3 marks each)

1 Three statements are provided here which define the terms– (a) sludge (b) sewage (c) wastewater

Pick out the correct definition for each of these terms.

(a) The settled solids that are removed in wastewater treatment with a scraper.

(b) Water from kitchen used for washing dishes.

(c) Wastewater released from homes, industries, hospitals and other public buildings.

2 Write three major characteristics which make water potable (safe for drinking).

Long Answer Type Questions (5 marks each)

1 Describe an activity to show the process that take place at the water treatment plant.

2 Think and suggest some ways to minimise waste and pollutants at their source, taking your home as an example.

____

____

ACTIVITY 1 (Jumbled Sentence)

Given below is a jumbled sequence of the processes involved in a wastewater treatment plant. Arrange them in their correct sequence.

(a) Sludge is scraped out and skimmer removes the floating grease.

(b) Water is made to settle in a large tank with a slope in the middle.

(c) Large objects like plastic bags are removed by passing wastewater through bar screens.

(d) Sand, grit and pebbles are made to settle by decreasing the speed of incoming wastewater.

(e) Wastewater enters a grit and sand removal tank.

ACTIVITY 2 (Word Identification)

Complete the following words:

(i) The colour of wastewater

__ __ A __ __ __ __ __ __ W __

(ii) A liquid waste

__ __ __ A __ __

(iii) An instrument used to remove oil and grease from wastewater

__ __ __ __ __ E __

(iv) The trees which absorb surplus wastewater rapidly.

__ __ __ __ __ Y __ __ U __

(v) A chemical which may kill microbes that help purify water

__ __ __ __ __ __ __ I __

ANSWERS

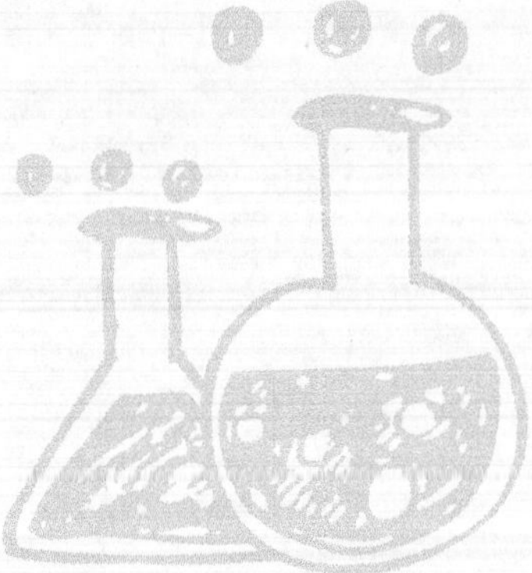

Answers

1. Nutrition in Plants

Worksheet 1

MCQs

1. (c) 2. (b) 3. (a) 4. (d) 5. (b) 6. (d)

Fill in the Blanks

1. (a) heterotrophs (b) photosynthesis
(c) Chlorophyll (d) cytoplasm
(e) Carbohydrates (f) nitrogen

True/False

1. (a) True (b) False (c) True (d) False
(e) False (f) False (g) True

Matching Type

1. (a)-(iv) (b)-(ii) (c)-(i) (d)-(iii) (e)-(iii)

Very Short Answer

1. Solar energy.
2. *A*-Nucleus, *B*-Cytoplasm, *C*-Cell membrane

Worksheet 2

Fill in the Blanks

1. (a) host (b) *Cuscuta*
(c) saprotrophic (d) algae
(e) Fertilisers /Manures (f) *Rhizobium*

True /False

1. (a) False (b) True
(c) True (d) False
(e) True

MCQs

1. (b) 2. (b) 3. (b)

Very Short Answer

1. (a) Mushroom, yeast
(b) Peas, *mung*, gram

Summative Assessment

MCQs

1. (a) 2. (b) 3. (b) 4. (a) 5. (b)

Very Short Answer

1. Nitrogen 2. Cactus
3. Starch 4. *Cuscuta*
5. Symbiosis

Activity

Autotrophs

(i) BHINDI (ii) GINGER
(iii) CARROT (iv) TULSI
(v) BANYAN

Heterotrophs

(i) CROW- OMNIVORE (ii) COW- HERBIVORE
(iii) ELEPHANT-HERBIVORE
(iv) BEE- HERBIVORE (v) MICE- OMNIVORE
(vi) FOX- CARNIVORE (vii) RABBIT- HERBIVORE
(viii) MUSHROOM- SAPROPHYTE

2. Nutrition in Animals

Worksheet 1

Matching Type

1. (a)-(iii) (b)-(i) (c)-(iv) (d)-(ii)

MCQs

1. (a) 2. (a) 3. (d) 4. (d) 5. (d) 6. (d)

Fill in the Blanks

1. (a) mouth, anus
(b) buccal cavity, small intestine
(c) sockets, gums
(d) back, front
(e) salts, water
2. (a) liver (b) gall bladder (c) fats
(d) glycerol (e) fatty acids

True/False

1. (a) False (b) False (c) False
(d) False (e) False (f) True
(g) False (h) False

One word answer

1. Oesophagus 2. Milk teeth
3. Glucose

Very Short Answer

1. (a) Small intestine, because digestion of food does not take place in the other three.
(b) Glycerol, it is the product of fat digestion
2. Diarrhoea

Worksheet 2

MCQs

1. (c) 2. (b)
3. (a)

True/False

1. (a) False (b) True
(c) True (d) False

Fill in the Blanks

1. (a) ruminant (b) caecum
(c) large intestine (d) cellulose
(e) bacteria (f) humans

Matching Type

1. (a)-(iv) (b)-(v) (c)-(i)
(d)-(iii) (e)-(ii)

Very Short Answer

1. Rumen is the first chamber of alimentary canal in ruminants, where food is stored and partially digested.
2. Pseudopodia 3. Food vacuole

Summative Assessment

MCQs

1. (c) 2. (a) 3. (a) 4. (c) 5. (b)

Very Short Answer

1. During mastication, salivary amlyase acts on starch of food and changes it into a sweet sugar.
2. Oesophagous
3. The set of 32 teeth that replaces the milk teeth is called the permanent teeth.
4. Energy is released.
5. Chocolates, sweets, soft drinks and other sugar products.

Activity

Across	Down
1. PANCREAS	2. *AMOEBA*
4. TONGUE	3. FAECES
5. ANUS	6. SIX
7. BILE	8. LIVER
10. VILLI	9. SALIVA
13. SOUR	11. COW
14. ACID	12. CUD

3. Fibre to Fabric

Worksheet 1

MCQs

1. (b) 2. (a) 3. (d)

True/False

1. (a) True (b) True (c) False (d) True
(e) True

Fill in the Blanks

1. (a) Good quality wool (b) Rampur bushair
(c) Carpet wool (d) Bakharwal
(e) Coarse wool (f) Patanwadi
2. (a) bacterium (b) anthrax
(c) sorter's disease (d) occupational
(e) hazards

Matching Type

1. (a)-(v) (b)-(ii) (c)-(iv) (d)-(iii) (e)-(i)

Worksheet 2

MCQs

1. (b) 2. (c) 3. (c) 4. (d) 5. (a)

True/False

1. (a) True (b) False (c) True (d) False
(e) True

Matching Type

1. (a)-(iv) (b)-(iii) (c)-(i) (d)-(ii)

Fill in the Blanks

1. (a) eggs (b) pupa
2. (a) reeling (b) protein
(c) cocoons (d) warm, bad

Very Short Answer

1. China 2. Mulberry tree
3. On mulberry leaves

Short Answer

1. Correct order - (e), (a), (d), (c), (f), (b)

Summative Assessment

MCQs

1. (d) 2. (a) 3. (c) 4. (b) 5. (b)

Activity

1. YAK 2. CAMEL 3. SHEEP

4. Heat

Worksheet 1

Fill in the Blanks

1. (a) 35°C (b) 37°C, vary
(c) – 10°C, 110° C (d) Kink

True/False

1. (a) False (b) False (c) True (d) True
(e) False (f) False (g) True

Matching Type

1. (a)-(iv) (b)-(i) (c)-(ii) (d)-(iii)

MCQs

1. (d) 2. (c) 3. (a) 4. (a) 5. (c)

Worksheet 2

Fill in the Blanks

1. (a) Conduction (b) Plastic, wood
(c) Sea breeze (d) Land breeze
(e) Radiation (f) Light, dark
(g) Reflected, absorbed

True/False

1. (a) False (b) False (c) True
(d) True (e) True (f) True
(g) True (h) False (i) True

Matching Type

1. (a)-(ii) (b)-(i) (c)-(iii) (d)-(iv)

MCQs

1. (c) 2. (b) 3. (a) 4. (b)
5. (b) 6. (c) 7. (c) 8. (a)

Summative Assessment

MCQs

1. (a) 2. (b) 3. (a)
4. (b) 5. (b)

Activity 1

Across
1. TEMPERATURE
5. CONDUCTION
6. INSULATOR

Down
2. CONVECTION
3. THERMOMETER
4. RADIATION

Activity 2

(a) CONDUCTOR (b) CELCIUS
(c) LANDBREEZE

5. Acids, Bases and Salts

Worksheet 1

Fill in the Blanks

1. (a) Lemon juice (b) Curd
(c) Amla (d) Tamarind
(e) Sugar (f) Grapes
(g) Common salt (h) Baking soda
2. (a) Vinegar (b) Formic acid
(c) Spinach (d) Grapes
(e) Citric acid (f) Curd
(g) Ascorbic acid

MCQs

1. (a) 2. (a) 3. (b) 4. (c)

True/False

1. (a) False (b) True (c) False (d) False
(e) True (f) False (g) True

Matching Type

1. (a)-(ii) (b)-(i) (c)-(iv) (d)-(iii)

Short Answer

1. (a) red (b) dark pink (c) red to blue
(d) blue (e) dark pink (f) red to blue
(g) dark pink

Worksheet 2

Fill in the Blanks

1. (a) salt, water, heat (b) hydrochloric acid
(c) slaked lime (d) acidic

True/False

1. (a) False (b) False (c) True (d) False

MCQs

1. (d) 2. (a) 3. (b)

Summative Assessment

MCQs

1. (a) 2. (b) 3. (b) 4. (a) 5. (c)

Activity 1

1. ACIDS 2. SOIL 3. BASIC 4. PINK

Activity 2

Across
2. NEUTRAL
4. BASE
7. RED

Down
1. INDICATOR
3. TURMERIC
5. ACIDIC
6. HEAT

6. Physical and Chemical Changes

True/False

1. (a) True (b) False (c) True (d) True
(e) True (f) True (g) True (h) False
(i) False (j) False

MCQs

1. (c) 2. (b) 3. (d) 4. (c)
5. (a) 6. (b) 7. (a) 8. (c)

Fill in the Blanks

1. (a) rusted (b) carbon dioxide
(c) chemical (d) oxygen, water
(e) Stainless steel (f) oxygen

2. (a) Chemical change
   (b) Physical change, cold water $\rightleftharpoons$ hot water
   (c) Chemical change
   (d) Physical change, whole chalk $\rightleftharpoons$ Broken chalk pieces
   (e) Physical change, ice $\rightleftharpoons$ water
   (f) Chemical change

Matching Type

1. (a)-(ii) (b)-(i) (c)-(vii) (d)-(v)
   (e)-(iv) (f)-(viii) (g)-(vi) (h)-(iii)

Very Short Answer

1. (a) $Mg + O_2 \longrightarrow MgO$
   (b) $MgO + H_2O \longrightarrow Mg(OH)_2$
2. $CO_2 + Ca(OH)_2 \longrightarrow CaCO_3 + \underset{\text{Water}}{H_2O}$

Activity 1

1. radiation 2. shield 3. pollution 4. chemical

Activity 2

Across
1. IRON
2. STAINLESS STEEL
4. CRYSTALLISATION

Down
3. MEDICINE
5. MAGNESIUM

7. Weather, Climate and Adaptation of Animals to Climate

Worksheet 1

MCQs

1. (a) 2. (b) 3. (b) 4. (c) 5. (c) 6. (d)

Fill in the Blanks

1. (a) weather (b) longer
   (c) Minimum (d) Weather
   (e) hot, high

True/False

1. (a) True (b) True (c) False
   (d) False (e) False (f) True

Matching Type

1. (a)-(iv) (b)-(iii) (c)-(ii) (d)-(i) (e)-(v)

One word Answer

1. Humidity
2. Rain guage
3. Millimeters (mm)
4. Thermometer
5. Celsius (°C)

Very Short Answer

1. Temperature, humidity, rainfall, wind speed, etc.
2. Sun
3. Hot and wet climate

Worksheet 2

True/False

1. (a) False (b) False (c) True (d) False

MCQs

1. (d) 2. (d) 3. (d) 4. (b) 5. (d)

Matching Type

1. (a)-(iv) (b)-(ii) (c)-(i) (d)-(iii) (e)-(v)

Examples of Regions

1. India, Malaysia, Indonesia and Brazil.
2. Iceland, Canada, Greenland, Sweden
3. Monkeys, apes, elephants, leopards
4. Reindeers, foxes, seals, penguins
5. Lions, tigers

Very Short Answer

1. Climate
2. (a) Siberian crane (b) Migratory bird (c) Winter

Summative Assessment

MCQs

1. (a) 2. (c) 3. (b) 4. (b) 5. (d)

Very Short Answer

1. Bharatpur and Sultanpur
2. South pole and North pole
3. Silver white mane which surrounds the head from the cheeks down to its chin.
5. Red-eyed frog and bird toucan.

Activity 1

(a) (i) CLIMATE (ii) POLAR
    (iii) THERMOMETER (iv) HUMIDITY

Activity 2

Tropical Rain Forest	Polar Region
Hot and Humid Climate	Penguin
Gorilla	Reindeer
Monkey	Greenland
Assam	Sun does not rise for six months
Day and night are almost equal in length throughout the year.	Winter temperature around – ° C
Western Ghats	

8. Winds, Storms and Cyclones

Worksheet 1

Fill in the Blanks

1. (a) reduced (b) lighter
   (c) heating (d) wind, land, ocean

True /False

1. (a) False (b) True (c) True
   (d) True (e) True

MCQs

1. (b) 2. (b) 3. (d)

Matching Type

1. (a)-(iii) (b)-(i) (c)-(iv) (d)-(ii)

Worksheet 2

True /False

1. (a) False (b) True (c) False
   (d) False (e) False (f) True

Matching Type

1. (a)-(ii) (b)-(iv) (c)-(i) (d)-(iii)

MCQs

1. (a) 2. (c) 3. (b) 4. (d)

Summative Assessment

MCQs

1. (a) 2. (d) 3. (a) 4. (c) 5. (b)

Activity 1

1. CYCLONE 2. TORNADO
3. HURRICANE 4. THUNDERSTOR
5. TYPHOON 6. LIGHTNING

Activity 2

Across
1. RAIN
2. CONTRACT
3. PRESSURE

Down
4. ANEMOMETER
5. WIND

9. Soil

Worksheet 1

True/False

1. (a) True (b) True (c) False
   (d) False (e) False (f) False

Fill in the Blanks

1. (a) topsoil (b) A-horizon
   (c) lesser, more (d) less
   (e) Bedrock (f) same
   (g) clay

MCQs

1. (c) 2. (c) 3. (d) 4. (c) 5. (c)

Matching Type

1. (a)-(vi) (b)-(iv) (c)-(i)
   (d)-(ii) (e)-(iii) (f)-(v)

Very Short Answer

1. The nature of any soil depends upon the rocks from which it has been formed and the type of vegetation that grows in it.
2. A-horizon or topsoil
3. Loamy soil = sand + clay + silt

Worksheet 2

True/False

1. (a) False (b) True (c) False
   (d) False (e) True (f) True

Fill in the Blanks

1. (a) soil moisture (b) evaporated (c) paddy
   (d) cotton (e) humus, fertile (f) roots

MCQs

1. (a) 2. (b) 3. (d) 4. (b)

Very Short Answer

1. $\frac{\text{Volume of water absorbed by soil}}{\text{Weight of soil}} \times 100$
2. Particle size

Short Answer

1. 10 minutes

Summative Assessment

MCQs

1. (b) 2. (d) 3. (d)
4. (b) 5. (b)

Very Short Answer

1. (a) Prevent deforestation
   (b) Increasing the green cover (vegetation)
2. 10 percent
3. Increasing the green cover (vegetation) on earth's surface to prevent soil erosion is called soil conservation.
4. Sugarcane and cotton
5. The dead plant parts get decomposed and enuch the soil by providing humus which forms the top soil or A-horizon.

Activity 1

(a) Humus, Sand, Water, Clay, Gravel, Weathering, Horizon, Percolation, Mineral, Plant, Erosion, Profile.

Activity 2

(i) HUMUS (ii) SOIL PROFILE
(iii) HORIZON (iv) LOAM
(v) WEATHERING (vi) PERCOLATION

10. Respiration in Organisms

Worksheet 1

Fill in the Blanks

1. (a) respire (b) oxygen (c) Yeast
   (d) muscle (e) breathe (f) diaphragm, ribcage

True/False

1. (a) True (b) False (c) True (d) True
   (e) True (f) True

MCQs

1. (c) 2. (c) 3. (c) 4. (b) 5. (a)

Matching Type

1. (a)-(ii, v, vi) (b)-(i, iii, iv)

Very Short Answer

2. Alcohol and CO_2 3. Water vapour 4. Smoking

Worksheet 2

Matching Type

1. (a)-(iii) (b)-(i) (c)-(iv) (d)-(ii)

MCQs

1. (c) 2. (b) 3. (a) 4. (c)

True/False

1. (a) True (b) True (c) False (d) False (e) False

Fill in the Blanks

1. (a) Earthworms, moist and slippery
   (b) blood vessels, oxygen, water
   (c) Dolphins, whales, upwards, blow holes

Respiratory organ

1. Lungs 2. Skin 3. Lungs

Very Short Answer

1. Gills
2. Energy, carbon dioxide and water.

Summative Assessment

MCQs

1. (c) 2. (c) 3. (b) 4. (a) 5. (a)

Very Short Answer

1. Sneezing releases germs (microbes) in air which may be inhaled by other people and infect them.
2. Blood helps to transport oxygen throughout the body.
3. Food is the source of energy for cells.
4. Because of rapid breakdown of food during physical activity which accelerates rate of breathing.
5. It brings extra oxygen to the lungs and helps us to keep awake.

Short Answer Type I

1. (a) The liquid in the test tube is alcohol
   (b) It is used for making wine and beer

Activity 1

(i) EXHALATION (ii) DIAPHRAGM
(iii) SPIRACLES (iv) NOSTRILS
(v) CARBON DIOXIDE (vi) GILLS
(vii) LUNGS (viii) RESPIRATION

Activity 2

(a) 'C'. The mice kept under the jar will breathe out CO_2 continuously increasing its amount in the bell jar.

(b) 'A' jar in which the CO_2 released during respiration is used by the plants during photosynthesis.

11. Transportation in Animals and Plants

Worksheet 1

MCQs

1. (a) 2. (c) 3. (c) 4. (d) 5. (d) 6. (a) 7. (b)

Matching Type

1. (a)-(i) (b)-(iv) (c)-(iii) (d)-(ii)

True/False

1. (a) False (b) True (c) False (d) False
   (e) True (f) True

Fill in the Blanks

1. (a) Arteries (b) veins (c) Veins (d) arteries
   (e) arteries (f) veins (g) Arteries (h) veins

One Word Answer

1. Plasma 2. Haemoglobin 3. WBCs
4. Capillaries 5. Arteries 6. Veins

Very Short Answer

1. Size of heart is almost the size of our fist
2. Sponges and *Hydra* 3. William Harvey

Worksheet 2

Fill in the Blanks

1. (a) blood (b) blood (c) blood (d) kidneys
   (e) blood (f) kidneys (g) blood

True/False

1. (a) True (b) True (c) False (d) False
   (e) True (f) True (g) True

MCQs

1. (b) 2. (b) 3. (c) 4. (c)

Matching Type

1. (a)-(iv) (b)-(iii) (c)-(i,ii) (d)-(iii)

Very Short Answer

1. 1-1.8 litres of urine
2. Because of the presence of salts in our sweat
3. (a) Oxygen (b) Urine (c) Fishes

Worksheet 3

Fill in the Blanks

1. (a) minerals (b) root hair
   (c) surface area (d) water
   (e) minerals (f) water
   (g) root hair (h) water
   (i) soil
2. (a) water, CO_2 (b) glucose
   (c) vessels (d) evaporation
   (e) Transpiration

MCQs

1. (d) 2. (b) 3. (a) 4. (c)

True/False

1. (a) Glucose – Phloem (b) Water – Xylem
   (c) Mineral nutrients – Xylem (d) Other sugars – Phloem
   (e) Oils, do not get transported

Very Short Answer

1. Because other parts of plant are unable to make food.
2. Xylem 3. Stomata

Summative Assessment

MCQs

1. (a) 2. (a) 3. (a) 4. (d) 5. (c)

Very Short Answer

1. 95 because heartbeat is equal to pulse rate.
3. The person will die due to toxicity in blood
4. Urea
5. (a) Exhalation-Lungs (b) Excretion-kidneys

Short Answer Type II

2. (b) *P*-Stomata
   Q-Xylem
   R-Phloem

Activity

(i) PHLOEM (ii) STETHESCOPE
(iii) PLATELETS (iv) ARTERIES
(v) TRANSPIRATION

12. Reproduction in Plants

Worksheet 1

MCQs

1. (a) 2. (d) 3. (a) 4. (c) 5. (d) 6. (c) 7. (c)

Matching Type

1. (a)-(iii) (b)-(ii) (c)-(i)

True/False

1. (a) True (b) False (c) True
   (d) True (e) False (f) True

Fill in the Blanks

1. (a) stem (b) leaf (c) roots (d) roots

One Word Answer

1. Rose 2. Potato 3. Fern

Very Short Answer

1. (a) Flowers
   (b) Rice
2. Sori in ferns are a cluster of sporangia (structure producing and containing spores) on the underside of its leaf.

Worksheet 2

MCQs

1. (b) 2. (c) 3. (b) 4. (c) 5. (b)

Fill in the Blanks

1. (a) zygote (b) fertilisation
   (c) embryo (d) seeds
   (e) fruit (f) female
   (g) male

Matching Type

1. (a)-II (b)-I (c)-IV (d)-III

True/False

1. (a) False (b) True
   (c) True (d) False
   (e) False (f) True

One Word Answer

1. Anther 2. Ovary
3. Stigma 4. Petals

Very Short Answer

1. (a) Corn, papaya and cucumber
   (b) Mustard, rose and Petunia
2. (a) Anther and filament
   (b) Stigma, style and ovary
3. (a) (i) Maple and (ii) *Madar* (aak)
   (b) None of these
   (c) (iii) *Xanthium*

Summative Assessment

MCQs

1. (c) 2. (c) 3. (a) 4. (b) 5. (a)

Very Short Answer

1. (a) Sexual reproduction (b) Asexual reproduction
2. (a) Sexual reproduction (b) Asexual reproduction
3. (a) Yeast (b) Bread mould
4. (a) Stamen (b) Pistil
5. (a) Male gametes (b) Female gametes

Activity 1

(i) SPORE (ii) CUCUMBER
(iii) URENA (iv) TURMERIC
(v) WALNUT

13. Motion and Time

Worksheet 1

Fill in the Blanks

1. (a) speed (b) distance, time
   (c) distance, time (d) periodic
   (e) Quartz (f) time period

True/False

1. (a) True (b) False (c) False (d) True (e) True
   (f) True (g) True (h) True (i) False

MCQs

1. (b) 2. (a) 3. (c) 4. (c)
5. (a) 6. (c) 7. (a) 8. (a)

Matching Type

1. (a)-(i) (b)-(viii) (c)-(vi) (d)-(v)
   (e)-(vii) (f)-(iv) (g)-(iii) (h)-(ii)

Worksheet 2

True/False

1. (a) True (b) False (c) True (d) False

Fill in the Blanks

1. (a) pie chart (b) straight line (c) line

MCQs

1. (d) 2. (b) 3. (a) 4. (c)
5. (b) 6. (c) 7. (a) 8. (a)

Summative Assessment

MCQs

1. (c) 2. (a) 3. (b) 4. (a) 5. (d)

Activity

The graph between point *B* and *C* indicates that Raghu is not in motion between this time interval as distance is constant here.

14. Electric Current and Its Effect

Worksheet 1

Fill in the Blanks

1. (a) positive, negative (b) cells
   (c) filament (d) glow, incomplete
   (e) wire

True/False

1. (a) True (b) True (c) True (d) False (e) False

MCQs

1. (c) 2. (b) 3. (d) 4. (b) 5. (d)

Matching Type

1. (a)-(vii) (b)-(v) (c)-(i) (d)-(ii)
   (e)-(iv) (f)-(vi) (g)-(viii) (h)-(iii)

Worksheet 2

Fill in the Blanks

1. (a) heating, magnetic (b) element
   (c) material, length, thickness (d) CFLs
   (e) utensils (f) high

True/False

1. (a) True (b) False (c) True (d) False
   (e) True

Matching Type

1. (a)-(ii) (b)-(iv) (c)-(vi) (d)-(xi) (e)-(vii) -(viii)
   (g)-(ix) (h)-(x) (i)-(v) (j)-(iii) (k)-(i)

MCQs

1. (a) 2. (c) 3. (a) 4. (c) 5. (d) 6. (b)

Summative Assessment

MCQs

1. (b) 2. (a) 3. (c) 4. (c) 5. (c)

Activity

Across
1. SOLENOID
3. MAGNET
5. FUSE
6. SYMBOL

Down
2. HEATED
4. BATTERY

15. Light

Worksheet 1

True/False

1. (a) True (b) False (c) True (d) True
   (e) False (f) False (g) True

Fill in the Blanks

1. (a) energy (b) plane mirror
   (c) mirror (d) real, inverted
   (e) virtual, erect (f) Real
   (g) virtual

Matching Type

1. (a)-(ii) (b)-(iv) (c)-(vi) (d)-(v)
   (e)-(iii) (f)-(i)

MCQs

1. (d) 2. (d) 3. (b) 4. (c)
5. (a) 6. (b) 7. (c)

Worksheet 2

True/False

1. (a) True (b) False (c) False (d) True
   (e) True (f) False

Fill in the Blanks

1. (a) smaller (b) diverges, converges
   (c) convex (d) focus
   (e) virtual (f) very small
   (g) white

Matching Type

1. (a)-(ii) (b)-(i) (c)-(iv) (d)-(v) (e)-(iii)

MCQs

1. (b) 2. (b) 3. (b) 4. (a)

Summative Assessment

MCQs

1. (c) 2. (b) 3. (b) 4. (c) 5. (c)

Activity

(a) LIGHT (b) MIRROR (c) LENS (d) DISPERSION

16. Water: A Precious Resource

Worksheet 1

MCQs

1. (a) 2. (b) 3. (c) 4. (c) 5. (d)

True/False

1. (a) True (b) True (c) True (d) False (e) True

Matching Type

1. (a)-(iii) (b)-(iv) (c)-(ii) (d)-(i)

Fill in the Blanks

1. (a) Groundwater (b) Evaporation (c) Condensation
   (d) Clouds (e) Transpiration (f) Infiltration
   (g) Precipitation
2. (a) dams (b) drought (c) floods
   (d) rain, melting (e) rains, crops

Worksheet 2

MCQs

1. (c) 2. (b) 3. (d)

Matching Type

1. (a)-(iii) (b)-(iv) (c)-(i) (d)-(ii)

True/False

1. (a) True (b) False (c) False
   (d) True (e) True

Fill in the Blanks

1. (a) hot (b) scarcity
   (c) workers (d) dry
   (e) rivers (f) harvesting
2. (a) taps
   (b) rainwater harvesting
   (c) eighteen

Summative Assessment

MCQs

1. (d) 2. (c) 3. (c) 4. (a) 5. (c)

Short Answer Type II

1. Correct order: (c), (b), (a), (d)
2. (b) Water table will fall drastically.
   (c) Clouds

Activity

(a) WATER CYCLE (b) AQUIFER
(c) BHUJPUR (d) JAHAZ WALI
(e) DRIP IRRIGATION (f) CHERAPUNJI

17. Forests: Our Lifeline

MCQs

1. (b) 2. (d) 3. (d) 4. (a) 5. (b) 6. (c)
7. (c) 8. (b)

Fill in the Blanks

1. (a) water purifying (b) home (c) shrubs
   (d) Soil (e) carbon dioxide
2. (a) bacteria (b) fungi
   (c) nutrients (d) carbon dioxide
   (e) water (f) plants

True/False

1. (a) True (b) False (c) True (d) False
   (e) True

Matching Type

1. (a)-(iii) (b)-(v) (c)-(iv)
   (d)-(i) (e)-(ii)

Choose odd one out

1. Lion, as it is not a scavenger
2. Kerosene, as it is not a forest product
3. Porcupine, as it is not a name of a tree

Very Short Answer

1. Canopy ⟶ Understorey ⟶ Shrub layer ⟶ Herb layer ⟶ Forest floor
2. By the droppings and footprints of animals.
3. (a) Cedar (b) Palm
   (c) Eucalyptus (d) Cinnamon

Short Answer

1. (a) Gum, wood, spices, oils
   (b) Mynah, kingfisher, koel, jungle crow
   (c) Monkey, bear, elephants, deer
   (d) Beetle, spiders, ants, millipede
4. (a) Transpiration and evaporation
   (b) The closed canopy and many layers of vegetation
   (c) Covered ground with dead and decaying matter
   (d) The root system

Activity

(i) AFFORESTATION (ii) FORESTS
(iii) CANOPY (iv) BISON
(v) HUMUS

18. Wastewater Story

Worksheet 1

MCQs

1. (a) 2. (d) 3. (c)

True/False

1. (a) False (b) False (c) True (d) True (e) True

Fill in the Blanks

1. (a) dysentery (b) sewage treatment (c) anaerobic
   (d) aeration tank (e) 97%

Matching Type

1. (a)-II-(iii) (b)-I-(i) (c)-III-(ii)

Very Short Answer

1. Waste Water Treatment Plant
2. Aeration, filtration and chlorination
3. Chlorine and ozone
4. (a) Nitrates, phosphates (b) Animal waste, urea
   (c) Phosphorus, nitrogen (d) Cholera, typhoid

Worksheet 2

MCQs

1. (c) 2. (c) 3. (c) 4. (d)

True/False

1. (a) True (b) False (c) True (d) True (e) False

Matching Type

1. (a)-(iv) (b)-(i) (c)-(ii) (d)-(iii)

Very Short Answer

1. (a) Oils do not kill microbes if thrown down in drains.
   (b) Common cold is not caused due to contaminated water.
   (c) Aeration tanks are not an onsite sewage disposal system.
2. Oxygen
3. Septic tank toilets

Summative Assessment

MCQs

1. (b) 2. (a) 3. (c) 4. (c) 5. (d)

Very Short Answer

1. Biogas and manure
2. They are underground pipes which carry away dirty drainage water and waste (such as from toilets).
3. Microorganisms decompose the organic matter present in sewage.
4. Vacuum toilets
5. Septic tank toilet

Activity 1

1. Correct sequence (c), (e), (d), (b), (a)

Activity 2

(i) BLACK BROWN (ii) SEWAGE
(iii) SKIMMER (iv) *EUCALYPTUS*
(v) CHLORINE